OBSCURITY

RYAN CLARKE

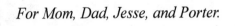

For Mom, Dad, Jesse, and Porter.

DANIEL BISHOP SAT WITH HIS feet dangling off the edge of the building, taking in a dangerous view of the Las Vegas Strip. He took a long drag of his cigarette. As he flicked it over the edge and watched it float out of sight, he allowed the smoke to escape his mouth and nostrils. Spotlights from the city's newest hotel, The Luxury, pierced the dark clouds above. Its lecherous owner, Richard Reynolds, was likely settling in for another night of cocaine and high-class hookers in the penthouse suite of the white marble eyesore. Safes full of millions in cash were hidden somewhere in the building's guts, but Daniel didn't know where.

Daniel's thoughts turned to *her*; smooth skin on his fingertips, the control he felt when he gripped her waist, the electric look she gave him when he came up for air. Black hair, pale skin, green eyes, hourglass figure, a penchant for melodrama, and a passion for the arts. She was difficult to argue with and easy to love.

No matter the hour, the lights of Las Vegas glimmered without rest, the streets teeming with people from all over the world, seeking a temporary escape from their worries to indulge in their vices. Vegas was enticing despite its dangers. That's why Daniel had wanted to move there in the first place: the woman and the city she thrived in—the light that drew him from the darkness all around.

With a groan, Daniel stretched his neck side to side and felt a soothing crack. He pressed his palms against the cold concrete and pushed himself up before pulling out his phone.

12:42 A.M.

ONE MISSED CALL: ANDRE GIBSON

He'd call Andre back later. Rain began to sprinkle on Daniel's head as he swung open the roof access door, taking the stairs down to the lobby of The Mirage. Weaving between slot machines and craps tables, the familiar smell of cigarettes and old carpet filled his nostrils. In the back corner of the casino, he arrived at a black door with silver accents and knocked twice.

Beady eyes emerged in the crack of the open door: Jerry, whose hands were shaking, his rat-like features even more pronounced when he appeared to be hiding. *These shakedowns are getting old*, Daniel thought. All these slimy businessmen were starting to look the same.

"Daniel, hey. Come on in," Jerry said, pushing his body into the doorway and making room to squeeze past. The room was filled with men counting money from the night's take so far. Bills whirred through electric counters and were folded in a semicircle, wrapped with a rubber band, and tossed into duffel bags. Daniel picked up a $100 bill and checked it out in the light.

"So, which of those bags is mine?" he said.

Out of the corner of Daniel's eye, Jerry's expression changed from a nervous smile to a confused puppy. Daniel wondered what rats called their babies.

"Wh-what do you mean, man?" Jerry said. "You already picked up your share for the month two weeks ago. The arrangement hasn't changed."

Daniel set the bill on the table and walked over to Jerry, leaning in close. "Come on, man. You and I both know you guys were light last time around. If you want me and Andre to keep bringing in these high rollers, you're going to have to start picking up your end."

Jerry's eyes widened. "But… but… Daniel… The economy ain't too good right now. And we're struggling just as much as the rest—"

Daniel slapped Jerry across the face. The casino manager squealed, falling back on the seat of his pants.

"Don't act like you're the only ones feeling the pinch," Daniel said, gesturing to the workers who had stopped what they were doing to watch the conflict. "Look at all the cash running through this place. I gotta make a living, too. And you were fucking light."

Daniel stepped over to one of the duffel bags, unzipping it to reveal an amount of money he would have killed for a decade ago. He zipped it back up and carried it out, letting the door slam behind him.

Eyes followed Daniel to the door, and a twinge of anxiety shot up his back. But this wasn't a robbery, and these weren't witnesses. This money was his, no matter how much Jerry whined. Near the front entrance of the hotel, steak cooking in the upscale restaurant overpowered the lingering smell of cigarettes from the casino. Daniel's stomach growled. He wanted to eat there but knew it would dredge up old memories like so many other places in the city. He and Gabby had gone there for one final blowout before the breakup.

Forget food. It was well past time to get liquored up. Rain buffeted the pavement as Daniel left The Mirage. A cool breeze brushed across the back of his neck, and his anxiety was carried away as fresh air relieved the tension in his stomach. Securing the bag with one hand and pulling his jacket over his head with the other, he took a left and strolled down Las Vegas Boulevard, stopping at the CVS to buy a fifth of vodka and a two-liter bottle of cherry soda. When Daniel made it back to his suite at the Venetian and into some dry clothes, he stretched himself out on one of the two queen beds.

Daniel pulled his phone out and called Andre. It rang twice before his best friend picked up, as he always did, in the aftermath of a late-night tryst.

"Yo, Dan," Andre said with a yawn. "What you gettin' into?"

"I'm at the Venetian with a bottle of Tito's that has your name on it. And a bag full of cash. Get over here and we can split it up. I've got a potential job for us, too."

"Aight then, lemme get dressed and I'll be over there," Andre said. A woman's voice mumbled in the background and Andre cleared his throat. "Okay, baby, time for you to get the fuck up outta here."

Andre hung up. Daniel smiled at his buddy's exploits as he set the phone down, but deeper inside him was an irrational streak of jealousy. It wasn't like Andre loved this girl—she was just another one on the list. And yet the idea of his friend having even a brief connection with a woman caused anger to bubble up inside Daniel. Why wasn't that him? Why couldn't he bring himself to sit at a bar and sweet talk a new woman into a night of intimacy or, easier yet, pay for it? Why was he letting Gabby win after their relationship was over?

Daniel got out of bed and poured himself a hearty serving of booze to go along with a meager splash of soda. He fired it down in a few seconds, leaving only the ice cubes to be greeted by another mixture of vodka and fizz.

He set his second serving on the nightstand between the two beds, propped up a few pillows, and leaned back against them, remote in hand. There wasn't shit on TV. He eventually settled on a Spanish-language movie with no subtitles. He couldn't understand a word but lost himself in the characters' emotions.

Three sharp knocks ended his fixation. He almost spilled his drink as he rushed to let Andre in. Checking the peephole first, he opened the door and dapped up his longtime pal.

The pair met when Andre moved to Daniel's neighborhood in Sacramento when they were both thirteen. Andre had grown up in South Florida in a small town, since consumed by the rising sea. "The Atlantis of the 'hood," he now called it. The two were troublemakers from the beginning. They hatched schemes to prank teachers and then graduated to lifting electronics from local stores. As they got older, the crimes became less petty. Five years after dropping out during their senior year of high school, Andre and Daniel picked up stakes and moved to Las Vegas, beginning a productive decade of robberies, car chases, and high-risk bets at the sportsbook.

"How we doin' Dan?" Andre asked, sauntering into the room. His dark skin shone under the bright lights of the entryway. It smelled like he'd just showered.

"Good. I'm only on my second drink so there's plenty left to fight over. You get that girl out of your hair?"

Andre sighed. "Yeah, but it took some work, bro. She was leechin' on me. Had to send her off with a wad of twenties. All it took was the feel of that green in her hands for that ho to dip out."

"Damn, man." Daniel handed Andre an empty glass. "Did she put you out? You still got enough for the tables next week?"

Andre glared at Daniel with faux disgust. "Man, I always got enough for the fuckin' tables. Don't play that shit, Dan. You just mad 'cause you lost your ass at the Bellagio last week."

"I didn't lose my ass," Daniel said. "I had an unfortunate string of losses, yes, but my ass remains intact. Now get *your* ass over here so I can pour you a drink."

Daniel gave Andre a 70/30 mix of soda and vodka—a far cry from the stiff ones he poured himself. Andre was a lightweight, he thought, so this was better for him anyway. And Daniel knew he needed a drink far more than Andre, given his recent breakup.

Andre took a sip and coughed. "Gahdamn, bro. This shit strong as a motherfucker."

"You want a little more soda?"

"Nah. I can handle it. Just watch yourself if I start acting crazy. It'll be your fault."

Daniel chuckled and lowered himself into the chair in the far corner of the room. Andre sat on the edge of the closest bed and squinted at the TV.

"The hell is this?" Andre asked.

"A Mexican drama filled to the brim with love, lust and murder. Get some culture in you, man. This is a classic of Spanish-language cinema."

A smile curled up from the edges of Daniel's lips. Andre turned to him with that signature fed-up look that had become a hallmark of their friendship.

"Don't tell me about no culture, cracker," Andre grunted. "I got more culture in my little fuckin' finger than you got in your whole body."

Daniel smiled even bigger and put his hands up.

"I'm messing with you, man," he replied. "I don't know shit about movies anyway. Turn that off, will you?"

Andre grabbed the remote and clicked it off. Daniel tossed the duffel bag to him and Andre sorted the cash out on the bed, setting aside what they owed and divvying up the portion he and Daniel could keep.

"So, what's this job you was talkin' about on the phone? I'm gettin' tired of the same old shit every week."

Daniel perked up. "Well, it just so happens I've got a job that will put a little spice in your life. You know Richard Reynolds, the wannabe mobster who owns that ugly ass new hotel, The Luxury? He's slipping up in his old age. People tell me he's getting suspicious of everybody around him. It's getting so bad that the guy is putting all his money in these big, old-school safes. He doesn't even trust the banks."

"Hot damn." Andre turned to Daniel and rubbed his hands together. "So we 'bout to rob this old fool blind?"

"That's where it gets tricky. We don't know where these safes are at, and for all we know they don't even exist. My guy on the inside tells me it's legit, but it's going to take some creativity on our end. Reynolds is a dangerous character. We're sticking our necks out on this one."

"This ain't a one-week proposition now, is it?"

"Not even close. This might take us months. But if this asshole is as rich as people in this town think he is, we're in for a major payday. Shit, we might even be able to retire off this; give up a life in the gutter for one the beaches in Santa Monica."

"Shit, man. That does sound nice. Find me a Puerto Rican girl with a fat ass, sip some Mai Tais by the ocean."

"Right," Daniel said. "But we can't think about that part right now. We've gotta find some way to get closer to Reynolds. My guy is close to him, but he doesn't know where these safes are located or how we might get inside them. Do you have any ideas?"

Andre paused for thought. Fiddling with one of the wads of cash, his shoulders twitched with a quick snort.

Daniel leaned forward. "What?"

Andre flashed his pearly whites. "What does every rich motherfucker in this town love more than all the money they got from clubs and casinos?" he asked. Daniel knew the answer before Andre had a chance to say it.

"You're saying we pry information out of him with, what, a hooker wearing a wire?"

"No, no, no. We could find a beautiful lady with a skill for this kinda thing. Somebody he might think is in love with him but she really workin' for us. You feel me? Then she could kill his ass once we got his money."

"Ah, I see." Daniel stroked his chin. "A black widow."

"She don't gotta be Black," Andre said with a chuckle. "We could find ourselves a White widow, Asian widow, Mexican widow—don't matter. Long as she can protect herself and can get us what we need."

"But…" Daniel paused. "She'll want a cut of the score, right?"

"Dan, my dude, don't get greedy on me now." Andre walked over to Daniel, placing a hand on his shoulder. "'Workers of the world unite.' Ain't that what Karl Marx said?"

"You've been reading Karl Marx?"

"Hell yeah," Andre said with visible pride, putting his hands on his hips. "I'm a socialist, motherfucker. I'm into all that wealth redistribution shit. World's been workin' too long for dudes like Reynolds and not for guys like us. That shit is generational. We gotta take it from 'em, and we need all the help we can get on that front, my guy."

Daniel had known Andre going on two decades, but this intense political rhetoric was new. *What could have sparked it?* Andre extended a hand to lift Daniel out of his chair. Daniel grabbed it and hugged his friend close while slapping him on the back. When they pushed apart and Andre returned to counting the money, Daniel took his drink to the window and thought about the prospects of unprecedented wealth. Bass thumped from a passing party bus on the streets below. The lights of hotels and clubs along the Strip maintained their eternal flash and flicker.

That anxious feeling shot up Daniel's back again. It felt like he was being watched, but it was just him and Andre in the room. Daniel peeked over his shoulder just to make sure. He caught Andre sniffing a fistful of the money.

"These bills got coke on 'em," he said. Daniel faked a laugh.

Doubt continued its steady creep into Daniel's mind. He and Andre had stolen from people who deserved it before, but few were as dangerous and well connected as Reynolds. They could go from binge drinking and chopping it up in hotel rooms to being dead and buried in the desert, just like that.

Daniel gulped and turned to Andre. "I think I might know somebody who could help us out."

2

SLOT MACHINES PINGED AND THE hum of conversation filled the casino hall. The smell of cheap cigars reminded Sarah of her father: most nights before bed, he would sit on the porch and gnaw on a stogey. It was a disgusting habit, she thought, and her mother couldn't have appreciated it. He didn't even bother to brush his teeth before kissing Sarah and her little brother goodnight. *Asshole.*

Sarah gestured to the blackjack dealer before saying, "Hit me."

His stubby, dark fingers placed the new card next to her seven of clubs and five of diamonds. It was a ten of diamonds. Sarah groaned, grabbed her clutch bag and strolled off. Her high heels clacked, and her ruby red dress reflected off the linoleum. She checked her watch: *11:34 p.m.*—the night was young. A cold drink to warm her up sounded like a plan, so she posted up at the edge of a nearby bar. She had a clear view of the door and nobody on either side of her. Her lingering nerves began to calm after the frustration of the card game.

It was raining hard outside. It reminded her of home; she tried to shake the thought. Oregon was far away from here, and she was far from the impressionable young soul searching for answers beneath a gray sky. Why was she getting so wistful about the past?

The bartender set a cosmopolitan in front of her and flashed a creepy smile. He either wanted a hefty cash tip or an illicit handjob.

Here's a tip, buddy: fuck off.

Sarah noticed the two men when they walked through the front door. A skinny, toned White guy in a black dress shirt and gray slacks, his brown hair brushed back but not slicked, with a chiseled jawline and an air of melancholy about him. Walking step for step with him was a Black guy in a pink button-up shirt and black dress pants, short haircut and a neatly trimmed beard. He oozed false confidence. She could tell by how he strutted.

The duo was headed her way. She realized as they approached that she'd met the White guy—Daniel—before. They had worked together on a small casino robbery a few months earlier. That was a mediocre endeavor, but she thought he was sweet. She liked his hair.

Sarah took a sip of her drink, pretending not to notice Daniel and his friend as they approached. They sat on the two stools to her left. Daniel ordered two rum and cokes and looked around. Was he really trying to play it off like he wasn't there for her?

"Hi there," he said, offering a handshake.

"We've met before, Daniel," Sarah replied. "Save the pleasantries."

Daniel introduced his associate. "This is Andre Gibson, my partner. Andre, this is Sarah."

Sarah nodded. Andre stood and approached her; she extended a hand and he kissed it like she was a nineteenth-century mistress searching for a husband at a fucking ice cream social. She snickered.

"Pleasure to meet you, *Monsieur Gibson*," she said, dripping with sarcasm. "Now what is it you guys want, exactly? I was enjoying this drink and I'd like to get back to it."

The bartender returned with Daniel and Andre's rum and cokes. They took a synchronized sip and gave each other a sideways glance before Daniel turned back to Sarah.

"We are looking for someone like you to help us with a job. It's good money, and someone of your, uh… talents might be able to seal the deal."

"Seal it with a kiss?" she scoffed. "Let me stop you right there, dude. I'm not your hundred-dollar whore and I'm not interested in whatever petty score you've got your eye on. My skills include slitting throats and handling firearms. Sorry to disappoint you."

Andre shifted in his seat. Daniel put a hand up as if to hold him back from interjecting.

"This isn't some small-time job," Daniel said. "We're talking millions—all for the taking from a notorious piece of shit. We think of you as an essential part of the team, and we'd be willing to give you forty percent of the take for your troubles."

Sarah kicked back her head and finished her drink. She took a long, observant gaze at the two men asking for her help, and their evident desperation brought her satisfaction. She cracked a smile.

"Forty percent, huh?" she asked. "If the money's as good as you say it is, I might be able to contribute to your little heist. What would you need from me if I were to say yes?"

Andre leaned onto the bar and lowered his voice.

"We need you to make some rich motherfucker fall in love with you. You don't even gotta sleep with him. Just get him fixated, and when the moment's right we take the cash right out from under him. Like Dan said, you're essential. That's why we wanted to give you a bigger piece of the pie, baby girl."

"First of all," Sarah snapped back, "I am far from your 'baby girl,' so turn off the charm for a few minutes and actually try talking to me like a business partner. Second, forty percent isn't enough for what you guys are asking. This is high-risk shit, gentlemen. I'm putting my ass on the line, and what happens if this doesn't go your way?"

Daniel put his hand on her shoulder. She flinched but turned her gaze to him slowly. Their eyes met. His were piercing blue, the reflection of the lights above him accentuating their rich color.

"We'll do forty-five, but only because we need you that badly," Daniel conceded. "This is Richard Reynolds we're talking about: scum of the earth. I saw what you did on the last job we were on and I know you can handle this. It's going to be hard, but if we pull this off, none of us will have to stay in Vegas much longer."

Sarah shifted in her seat and turned her body toward him, crossing one leg over the other.

"Maybe I like it here," she said.

"Sure you do," Daniel said. "So, will you join us for a night-cap to discuss details, or are you content to spend the rest of your night with that creep who poured us these weak-ass drinks?"

Sarah glanced over at the bartender. He wiggled his fingers in a strange wave and flashed a toothy smile behind his handle-bar mustache. She pulled out $40 and tossed it on the counter— enough for the three of them plus a decent tip.

"Let's go," she said.

Daniel, Andre and Sarah left the casino. Flashing lights reflected off the puddles forming on the street outside the front entrance. They stood underneath the massive stone awning where cabs and rideshares picked up passengers. Andre gave the valet his ticket, and Sarah felt anxiety in her chest. A gunshot rang out amidst the steady stream of rain. Glass shattered behind her. It was hard to breathe, and everything slowed down.

Fight or flight kicked in full throttle. She reached to the inside of her leg and pulled out a tiny concealed 9mm pistol. She knocked the valet out of the way and took cover behind his desk, firing a round toward the assailant that missed high. Sarah soon realized the gunman was leaning out the window in the backseat of a Range Rover. *What a fucking idiot.*

Sarah crouched down behind the desk as bullets whizzed past her, shattering more windows. Peeking around the corner of her cover, she spotted Daniel and Andre hiding behind a silver Mercedes, guns drawn, arguing about something. The gunman was still leaning out of the car, flailing with reckless abandon. She figured even this bozo wouldn't leave himself exposed for long, so she stood and fired three rounds at him. They struck his chest, stomach. and the bottom right corner of his jaw. *That'll do the trick.* His mangled corpse slumped over the edge of the car window, and the gun fell from his hands to the pavement.

Sarah ran to the center of the street and grabbed the dropped gun. The car screeched off as the gunman's body thumped against the side door. Blood gushed from his wounds and stained the car. As the vehicle picked up speed and turned the corner, someone pulled the stiff inside and rolled up the window. She couldn't make out the license plate or any faces beyond that of the deceased—who was as generic as heavyset White guys come.

She turned back toward the Mercedes.

"Get in," Daniel yelled from the passenger's seat. Andre was driving.

Sarah sprinted to the car and threw open the back door before diving in. Andre sped off before she could close it, but the sharp right turn he took did the job for her. Heavy breathing filled the vehicle as they sped down Las Vegas Boulevard. The bullets had left unsightly gashes in the otherwise pristine leather seats, and the doors were peppered with them. She examined her newfound compatriots who appeared to be unharmed by the debacle.

Nothing but gasps for breath until the group was off the Strip. Finally, Sarah worked up the mental energy to say something.

"You guys know those jagoffs?"

Daniel turned back to her, sweat beading on his forehead.

"No idea," he said. "Couldn't tell if they were coming for us or you. Got anything you need to tell *us* about?"

"I don't leave loose ends," she said. "So, think real hard about who it is you might have pissed off, and count yourselves lucky it's only this overpriced mid-life crisis that took the brunt of the beating."

Andre perked up from his seat. "The fuck you talkin' 'bout? No such thing as overpriced with a ride like this, baby. And how do I know it ain't your fault that it got more holes in it than that Shia LaBeouf movie?"

"Like I said, I don't have any loose ends," Sarah said. She took a moment to think. "Could this be that Reynolds character? The one you want me to help you guys rob? Think he got wind of what you guys are planning?"

"No chance," Daniel cut in. "Only the two of us had talked about it before we approached you, and that was last night."

More silence as the trio's breathing finally slowed. On the outskirts of downtown Vegas, Andre pulled into an autobody shop that hadn't been active in years—no lights on that Sarah could see, with paint chipped all over the cream-colored exterior walls.

Andre put the car in park and whipped out his phone. It rang twice before he hung up. An automated chain link gate opened, along with a garage door. Sarah observed a large Hispanic man wearing overalls over a white T-shirt. His arms were crossed, and he was shaking his head. He was losing his hair and sported a thick mustache and scraggly beard. His face sank with disappointment as Andre rolled the window down.

"Andre, *primo*, what have you done?" the man asked, observing the fresh scars all over the Mercedes.

"It's nothin' a little elbow grease won't fix, right Gus?" Andre replied.

Gus sighed.

"Get out, I'll take it off your hands," he said. "There's a loaner in the parking lot. Keys are in the glove box. I'll have this one back to you next week."

"My man," Andre said, slapping hands with Gus before turning the car off. He, Daniel and Sarah lifted themselves out of the car and checked for bullet wounds. Sarah's dress was torn slightly along her right leg, but she had plenty more in her closet. She wasn't working again tonight, anyway.

Making their way through the dark, tattered auto shop and out the back door, Sarah spotted their new ride: a significant downgrade from the Mercedes but refreshingly free of bullet holes. It was a Toyota from the 90's with plenty of wear and tear, and fuzzy dice hanging from the rearview mirror. They took their time getting in, and Sarah took shotgun this time around. Daniel got behind the wheel as Andre jammed himself into the backseat, knees pressing against the back of the driver's seat.

"Yo, Dan, can you move that shit up?" he asked.

"It's stuck," Daniel said through a grunt.

"Fuck it," Andre said, tossing the seatbelt aside and lying on his back across the width of the car. He weaved his fingers together across his chest and closed his eyes before taking a deep breath.

"So, where are we going now, my knights in shining armor?" Sarah said in a sarcastic tone.

"Not back to the Strip, that's for sure," Daniel said. "Too hot after what just went down. I've got a little place near Henderson we could lie low in for a while."

Daniel paused and stared at Sarah, his blue marble eyes seeming more sincere than desperate.

"Are you still in on this?" he asked.

"Well, I never technically agreed to anything," Sarah replied. "But what you guys said before the bullets started flying had me intrigued. And after tonight's events, I figure I'm stuck with you two dipshits for the time being; might as well make the most of it."

Daniel smiled and turned the keys. After some coaxing, the engine came to life.

3

WATCHING MEN DIE CAN GET old after a while. When the method of execution almost never changes, it starts to feel like a chore. Reynolds yawned and checked his watch under the minimal light in the dark alley. He had trouble seeing the numbers.

"Hurry up," he said to his henchman. "I don't have all night."

Martin "Big Marty" Fleck tightened the wire's grip around his victim's throat. A zip tie bound the man's wrists behind his back, preventing the poor sap from freeing himself. Still, he struggled like a landlocked fish. The muscles in his neck contracted, and the veins in Big Marty's fists pulsated as he pulled back with all his strength. Reynolds remained stone faced as the sounds of gurgles and dragging feet filled the air. Finally, the guy went limp, and Big Marty dropped his body to the pavement. His chest and head hit the ground with a wet thud—it had rained all last night, and it smelled like more was on the way.

"Find a comfortable dumpster for our friend, here," Reynolds said. "I'm done for the day."

Reynolds used his cane to steady himself and meandered over to the body. He looked down at the man and smiled.

"That'll teach ya to pay your debts, fuckwad," Reynolds said, leaning closer to the corpse. "What's that? You're sorry?"

Reynolds stood up and smiled at the band of thugs he had brought along for the killing.

"You hear that, boys? He's sorry. I guess we blew this one, huh?"

They all stared down at the pavement and waited for their next order. Reynolds reveled in the moment and gestured to his personal security, Oleg, that it was time to go. The pair walked in one direction while the rest of the crowd scattered. Reynolds could hear Marty dragging the body and struggling with the dead weight. *A guy that big and strong can't even handle this? Maybe he needs to cut back on the trips to the buffet.*

When Reynolds and Oleg reached The Luxury, Reynolds's recently minted project on the Strip, he noticed two workers behind the counter chatting. Reynolds stopped and held his hand up, forcing Oleg to stop in his tracks. His cane tapped on the floor along with his heavy footsteps as he approached the counter. The staff heard him before they saw him, and they stopped mid-conversation to straighten themselves up and force smiles. Reynolds leaned on the counter and shook a wrinkly finger at the young Hispanic workers in vests and bowties.

"You fucking wetbacks better be speaking English if you're chatting it up on my time," he grumbled. Their heads were lowered to protect themselves from his wrath. "Now, which one of you is going back out on the street where your kind belongs?"

They remained silent. The more experienced of the two—her nametag said Rosa—spoke up. The young man she was chatting with remained silent.

"We are so sorry, Mr. Reynolds. We'll get right back to work. No problem here."

"There better not be," Reynolds spat back. "Or I'll call *la migra* on your asses, *comprende*?"

They both nodded. Reynolds glared before moving along. If he were in political leadership, people like that wouldn't be allowed to work in places like this. But they were cheap labor and didn't ask questions. *Their only saving grace.*

As Reynolds followed Oleg through the lobby, he took in the sights of his crown jewel: a centrally located fountain in the lobby with statues of nude women, all the gritty details etched into each of them, just how he liked it. Above the fountain was a crystal chandelier that glittered beneath the lights. Marble floors wrapped around the fountain and toward the main elevator bay, where his personal elevator waited between the two civilian ones. Oleg turned a key, and the doors opened, revealing a spotless chrome interior with gold handrails at equal height with Reynolds's waist. He leaned against one in the back as the elevator doors slid closed.

"Find yourself in any good pussy lately, Oleg?"

Oleg stared forward and replied with a solemn, "No."

"Damn shame," Reynolds said, pretending there was some kind of camaraderie between himself and his subordinate. "Been a while for me, too. But I've got an excuse: I'm old! You're a young, strapping lad who's probably got a big old pecker swinging between his legs. Uncircumcised?"

Oleg turned his head and glared at his boss. "I'm married."

"I know that. I'm just messing with you, big guy. Don't act so serious. You Russian guys are always so *intense*, like the whole world is at fault for your daddy's failed potato farm. Lighten up, man. You're not on the Eastern Front, and there aren't any bread lines on Las Vegas Boulevard."

Oleg didn't react. The elevator pinged, and they arrived at Reynolds's suite. Smooth jazz was already playing on the speakers. A bucket of ice with a champagne bottle sat on the coffee table. Reynolds kicked off his shoes, removed his jacket, and handed it to Oleg. He limped, cane-free, over to the plushy couch and sank into it, putting his feet up on the table next to the bottle.

"Oleg, before you go, can you pop this bottle for me?" Reynolds asked as Oleg hung up his coat. "And bring over a glass. They're in the cupboard."

Reynolds closed his eyes and leaned back. When he opened them again, Oleg was in front of him, holding the bottle of champagne. He pressed his thumb on the cork before it popped off, and a bit of foam spilled into the glass before a steady stream of the good stuff. He placed the bottle on the table and handed the glass to Reynolds in silence.

"Thanks, big guy," Reynolds said, reaching into his pants pocket for a wad of $100 bills. "You're good to go. Here's a few hundred bucks for the tables or a nice young mistress to slob on your knob—Lord knows you need it. Send me some pictures if you go that route."

Oleg gave another blank stare as he took the cash, pocketed it, and headed for the exit.

Alone at last. Reynolds loosened his collar and took a deep breath. Nothing to tend to but an ice-cold glass of celebration for a night of hard work. In the old days, he was right in the thick of it, swinging baseball bats and tire irons. *But with old age comes delegation*, he thought. No use straining himself with the tough stuff anymore, as much as he missed the opportunity to crack skulls and wrap his fingers around the necks of those who wronged him.

The music on the speakers cut out. It was silent in the room for a moment before it kicked back on, and Reynolds set his glass down in anger.

"Who the fuck set this shit up?" he asked, pushing himself out of his seat and making his way over to the speaker. "Skipping in the middle of a fucking song. Like I got this shit at a fucking garage sale. Give me a break."

Reynolds checked the system for an issue. There didn't appear to be anything wrong. He turned it up a couple notches before turning back toward the couch.

The bottle was back in the ice bucket. *Did I put it there?* He shook the thought from his mind and sat back down, resting his eyes once more as the sounds of a luxurious saxophone filled the room. Reynolds thought about that man's face while Marty had choked him out; eyes bugged out, bloodshot as they searched for something or someone to help him; the sound his body made when it hit the ground; the empty gaze as he lay there without a soul. In his mind, Reynolds saw the eyes go from staring straight ahead to looking right up at him. A hand reached up from the pavement and grabbed his leg.

Reynolds woke with a kick that drove his toe into the bottom of the coffee table.

"Ahh, fuck!" He briefly panicked, thinking the bottle and ice would be knocked over, but now they were on the TV stand, way over by the speaker. Pain rushed to his foot and he grumbled. Sweat ran down his face as he came back to reality.

"Okay, time for bed, old boy."

The ice bucket fell to the floor and the bottle shattered on impact. Reynolds jumped. Ice cubes slid across the marble to his feet, and a pool of champagne, glass, and ice formed in front of the speakers. The sound of footsteps began near the puddle and echoed farther and farther away, disappearing down the hallway.

Reynolds was frozen, shaking, unsure what to do next.

"Who's there?" he yelled. Silence. The music had stopped. "Oleg, you getting back at me, you Russian fuck? I won't joke about your foreskin anymore, I promise."

Even Reynolds didn't laugh at his attempt to fill the air with humor instead of fear. He sat back down and grabbed the phone to call housekeeping. Somebody needed to clean this shit up, and he was getting tired of being alone.

The phone rang seven times, longer than he'd like, and it sounded like someone picked up on the other end. Reynolds was expecting the voice of the girl at the front desk who he'd just berated, but the line was silent.

"Hello?" he said. "It's Richard. I need someone up here to clean up a mess."

More silence. Then faint breathing. It grew louder each time it drew in. Reynolds leaned to the right and stared down the dark hallway. The door to his bathroom slammed closed. The breathing stopped, and the call cut out. A droning dial tone was all that was left. Reynolds put the phone down and got up, stumbling toward the hallway.

He stopped himself at the kitchen and pulled open a small drawer to reveal a silver pistol sitting on a red pillow with yellow accents. He grabbed it, cocked it, and kept limping. The bathroom door was open, and the light was on. Reynolds raised the weapon and took measured steps in that direction.

Turning the corner into the bathroom, he whipped the gun toward the shower only to see his own warped reflection in the textured glass. His sweaty finger twitched on the trigger as he turned left toward the toilet, then left again to the sink and mirror. Nowhere for anyone to be hiding. *Am I losing my shit?*

He took a heavy breath in and let it out slowly. One more through his nose and out his mouth. He lowered the gun before setting it on the sink. Observing himself in the mirror, Reynolds saw the age below his eyes. Bags were sagging lower by the day, and wrinkles covered his pale forehead, his neck drooping with the appearance of a turkey gizzard. His eyes remained a deep shade of brown, but they'd yellowed around the edges from all the smoking, as had his teeth. He pulled his gray locks back from his face and ran his fingers through them. At least he wasn't bald.

Reynolds turned on the faucet and splashed water on his face. When he lifted his head, a man in a red suit jacket, black shirt and black pants was standing by the shower behind him. His skin was pale, his black hair was slicked with oil, and his eye sockets were empty and oozing blood. He flashed a sinister smile with his chin against his chest.

Reynolds reached for the gun, turned, and fired. It shattered the glass door of the shower and left a hole in the wallpaper.

The man wasn't there.

"Fuck this," Reynolds said. His hand was shaking, the gun rattling between his fingers. He lifted it and pressed it to his temple, cocked it, and screamed.

"Leave me alone!" he bellowed. "Get out of my head!"

The lights in the bathroom went out, then back on. Reynolds lowered the gun, sank to the floor and pushed himself against the wall. He crossed his arms over his knees and buried his face in them, crying while his shoulders shook. For weeks, this paranoia had plagued his mind, but never before had he seen this person— *thing?*—show up anywhere other than his nightmares. He lifted himself up and nearly fell as his bad leg struggled to balance his weight. He brought the gun with him and rushed to his bedroom, peeling off his clothes and jumping under the covers like a child. The gun and his cell phone sat on his nightstand, the light of the lamp reflecting off the weapon's chrome surface. He turned the lamp off and rolled over, one hand under the pillow and another clutching the sheet over his head.

Reynolds was just about to fall asleep when his bedroom door creaked. He tossed the sheet aside. The door was wide open. Something whispered in his ear.

"Room for one more?"

4

THE ENGINE CHURNED AND KICKED to a merciful
stop as Daniel put the car in park. Gus's loaner had
barely made the journey to Henderson. Andre jerked
awake in the backseat and hit his head on the roof.

"Ah, shit," he said, rubbing the top of his skull. "We here?"

"Yep," Daniel replied, pulling the keys out of the ignition.

They left the car parked a few blocks down the road from
the safehouse. Rain fell fast and hard, soaking through Daniel's
clothes. He ignored the cold feeling on his skin and worried
about whether they were followed.

Andre pulled his jacket over his head. Sarah threw her head
back, letting the raindrops fall on her face and smear her eyeshadow. She took long strides and held her arms wide, taking
it all in. Her brown hair darkened as the rain ran through it, her
collarbone collecting water droplets that trickled down her chest.

Daniel thought she must be washing herself from the sins of
the night. It couldn't have been her first kill, but it was a gruesome one. He remembered how the shooter's body floundered
out the car window, half his jaw missing, blood pouring to the
pavement from the orifices she had created with bullets; all while
he and Andre were bickering about who should come at the guy

from which angle. She had it taken care of, striking while her victim was exposed.

Sarah caught him staring at her. Mascara running down her face and rain soaking through her red dress, she smiled for the first time all night. It lit a fire inside him. Even as Andre's heavy steps splashed behind them, it felt like he and Sarah were alone. He wanted to reach for her face and bring it close, kissing her in the rain. But he thought better of it. Not only would it mix business with pleasure, but who knows if she'd even stick around? He'd just be another one on her list of spurned lovers with empty pockets, or worse: an opened throat or a hole in the back of the head. Why hadn't he noticed her free spirit the last time they worked together?

"I love the rain," Sarah said. "We don't get enough of it around here."

"Nah," Andre said from underneath his jacket. "This shit sucks. I just got a haircut on Monday. I'll be lucky if this don't mess my shit up. I can't get it wet."

The trio approached the safehouse and sheltered underneath the awning over the front porch. Sarah shook her hair and pulled it back, wringing the moisture out onto the deck. Andre used the front window to check his hair. Daniel climbed up the banister at the front of the porch, flipped up a shingle, and pulled out the key. He hopped back down and turned the lock, jiggling the handle as he forced open the aging door.

He flicked on the lights and observed the sorry shape the place was in: dusty floors, cobwebs lining the hallway to the living room, a kitchen with dirty dishes in the sink attracting flies, a couch with a huge gash in one of its cushions. There was a clean rectangle on the wall where a flat-screen TV used to be. Daniel definitely hadn't been here in a while.

"Nice place you got here," Sarah said. "Now, if I want a

urinary tract infection, should I use the upstairs bathroom or downstairs?"

Andre sank into the couch, and dust puffed into the air around him. He started coughing and grimaced as he got up and stumbled away.

"No bathroom down here," Daniel said. "Let me check the one upstairs."

Daniel headed for the staircase. She followed him. Her high heels tapping on the hardwood behind him created a knot in his stomach. He thought about arriving at the bathroom and pushing her up against the wall before tearing off her wet clothes. He gulped as they turned the corner to the bathroom and flicked the lights on. To his surprise, it was relatively spotless. Whoever had been squatting here either cleaned the bathroom or didn't come upstairs at all.

Her hand brushed across his shoulder, sending chills down his spine.

"I'll take it from here," she said in a sultry voice, shutting the bathroom door behind her. Daniel stood outside and took a deep breath before letting out a massive exhale. He headed back downstairs to find Andre sitting in the backyard, smoking a cigarette in one of Daniel's lawn chairs. Another chair was set up next to him with a beer on the table between. The rain had ceased—save for a few leftover sprinkles—and the horizon was clear.

Daniel lowered himself into the lawn chair and leaned back, groaning to release all the pressures of the day. He took a swig from the beer. Still good, somehow. He wondered where Andre found it in the disheveled remains of the house.

"That girl is somethin' else, ain't she?" Andre said.

Daniel had just allowed his mind to wander to other subjects, and now he was thinking about her again. She was upstairs, in the shower, naked and waiting. He took another sip of beer.

"Yeah. You think she's up for this job?"

"No doubt. She's the real deal, man. She shot that motherfucker at the casino three times when we didn't even get one off. She don't fuck around."

Daniel nodded. Andre offered him a cigarette, but he declined.

"I'd hate to see her get mixed up in some sketchy shit," Daniel said. "What if Reynolds figures out the ruse? Then her blood is on our hands, and we're left with jack shit."

"Dan, my dude, you don't need to worry about her. She can handle herself. You don't gotta protect her, no matter what that primal shit bouncin' around in your head tells you. And you don't gotta worry about her fuckin' him, neither. She'll make him work for it, and by then, we'll all three be high-tailin' it outta here with his cash."

"I'm not worried about that," Daniel insisted. "It's her job to be the honey pot. It's just… the more I think about it, the more I worry about things going south. Nobody has tried something like this on Reynolds before. What if he catches wind and has someone kill her? Then they come after us?"

Andre leaned forward in his chair and reached out to Daniel, patting him on the knee and handing him his beer.

"Dan, you're overthinking it. Besides, this was your idea, and it's gonna work. I got no doubt in her, or you, or me doing our jobs. When we're done, this motherfucker won't know what hit him. Beaches in Santa Monica, Dan—that's all ya gotta think about. When we're crackin' the safe, think about them beaches. When we ace one of his guards, wiggle your toes in the sand. When you get your hands on that cheddar, imagine where it's gonna go. You feel me?"

Daniel took another deep breath and finished off the beer.

"Yeah, man. You're right. I'm just anxious is all."

"And you got a right to be, my guy. This is some precarious shit. We fuck this up and you're right: we're done for. But we can't be thinkin' about all that. We just gotta focus on tellin' Sarah what her job entails."

Andre pointed up at the sky.

"Take a look at them stars, bro. We can't even see them shits in downtown Vegas. Take a moment, meditate on that, and we can get down to business once Miss Thang comes back down here."

Daniel absorbed the gravity of Andre's words. Stars speckled the black void above them, each flickering in varied levels of brightness. One in particular caught his eye as it flashed brighter than the rest. He wondered if it was still alive—or if the light meeting his eyes was from a long-dead gaseous mass, burst into the vast vacuum of space, leaving its nearby planets cold and dark. *It's easy to think about the size of the universe and feel insignificant*, he thought. The problems of the day for everyone, criminal or otherwise, seemed fickle in the grand scheme of things. *But the perspective gained can also make you feel like there's a point to all this shit*, Daniel thought.

It's the only way this job made sense. His initial reason for pursuing this was a chance at happiness, at peace. The money could fill part of the hole inside him, and leaving Vegas would fill the rest. But every second spent with Sarah since the shootout made Daniel wonder what he really wanted.

"Maybe I like it here."

Maybe he did too. The thrill of living on the jagged edge kept his blood pumping. But the chance of a fall grew greater by the day. His stomach churned again as he snapped out of his stargazing trance. Andre was no longer sitting next to him, and Daniel panicked for a moment before turning around to see him doing dishes in the kitchen.

Daniel lifted himself out of the lawn chair and returned to the house. As he closed the sliding glass door, he turned around to observe Sarah coming down the stairs. She was wearing his *Star Wars* T-shirt along with baggy basketball shorts that were hardly form-fitting on her normally striking curves. Still, there was something sexy about this look. She was wearing sandals (*Where'd she get those?*) and had her hair in a ponytail. She wasn't wearing makeup, and it didn't matter. Her face was angelic, pristine, not a pock mark or mole in sight.

"You're out of hot water," she said. "But I can't say I'm surprised, given the rest of this place."

"Sorry about that," Daniel replied. "Can I get you something to drink?"

"Just water is fine." She pulled up to the dining room table. Daniel grabbed a plastic bottle from the fridge and one for himself, too.

They sat together and waited while Andre finished up the dishes. He tossed the last one in the dishwasher along with a soap pod and turned it on. It gurgled to life and finally churned along as he dried his hands and approached the table. He sat in the wooden chair next to Daniel, and it collapsed, taking him to the floor with it.

"Fuck!" Andre yelped. "God damnit, Dan. This place is a shithole."

Sarah couldn't contain her laughter. Daniel had his face in his hands, laughing too, and through his fingers, he could see her chuckling. It made him smile even bigger. Andre collected himself out of the remnants of the chair and stood, hands pressed on the table. He shook it a bit to make sure it was sturdy. Daniel patted him on the back, and Andre glared at him.

"Alright, so let's get down to business," Daniel said to Sarah. "We know that Reynolds has been spending a lot of time at his biggest hotel, The Luxury, in a penthouse suite designed specifically for him. He lives there alone, which means nobody else could get between you two if you catch his eye."

"So why don't I just kill him?" Sarah asked in an earnest tone.

Andre and Daniel shot each other a glance.

"It's not that simple," Daniel said. "A guy like this gets killed, he's got all kinds of fail-safes to make sure whoever did it gets flayed in the fucking street. He's got security cameras all throughout that place, and there's no way out of there without being caught on one of them. Besides, we need information that only he has. With paranoia comes isolation, and lately, he's isolated himself and his secrets to that fucking penthouse."

Andre leaned forward to speak, and the table creaked.

"And we want him to know somebody took this money from him when it's all over. No use stealin' from the rich if they ain't forced to live a new lifestyle. This revolution ain't violent; at least, not in that way."

"Fair enough," Sarah said. "But how am I gonna get him to trust me? He's probably got gold diggers hanging onto him for dear life every time he goes anywhere."

"That's the thing," Daniel said. "He has nobody in his life right now. He's old and alone, and from what I've been told, he is desperate for a companion, even with how paranoid he's been lately. All you need to do is set yourself up somewhere he'll be, and make him feel like you're worth it…"

"*Like* I'm worth it?" she said, forming a wry smile. "You don't think I'm worth it?"

"No, no," Daniel said. "It's not like that. I mean, you're gorgeous, but you need to really capture his attention. Disarm him. Make him think you have him figured out like nobody else does. Wrap him around your little finger and keep him there."

Andre chuckled. "You ain't gonna make her use her fingers on him, are ya Dan?"

"Shut the fuck up," Daniel said, refusing to look in Andre's direction as he cackled. Sarah seemed to appreciate the joke.

"Okay," she said, her hazel eyes moving from Andre to Daniel. "Where do I meet him?"

"There's a high-rollers' blackjack table in one of the back rooms that he plays every Friday night. The cards are always stacked in his favor. It's kind of sad, actually: the dealer starts to worry if the boss isn't up big. But this time, we've paid her off and offered her protection, and she's going to stack the game in your favor. That will grab Reynolds's attention."

"Do I get to keep the money I win?"

"That money is irrelevant with what we'll take from this job. He'll be frustrated that he lost but enamored with you by the end of the game. Sweet talk him. Tell him he played a great game. I don't need to tell you what to say—just use your best judgment. And once you convince him to let you come upstairs, keep the conversation going. If he makes a move, hold him off, tell him you want to wait until your next date to get physical."

"And what if I get to that date and he starts trying to get frisky? Then can I gut him?"

"We ain't worried about that right now," Andre said. "On this first round, we just need ya to put a bug in that penthouse, somewhere even his best guys won't see it. And don't let them cameras catch you doing that shit, neither."

Andre pulled a listening device out of his pocket and placed it on the table, pointing to his ear. Sarah examined the device and put it in, making adjustments until it wasn't visible. She modeled it for Daniel and Andre before taking it back out.

"We know he's been ordering his goons around and holding meetings in that room lately," Daniel said. "If we can pick something up about where those safes are—or how we might get into them without needing to bust them open—that's key intel. Make him wait a week to see you again; that will give us enough time to collect as much as we can. If we don't have something we can use, we'll have you try and pry it out of him later on."

"I see," she said, putting the device in her clutch bag. "So, when's the card game?"

"Nine p.m. tomorrow," Andre said. "Dan's got someone on the inside, so you just gotta tell security your name and they'll wave ya through. Then all ya gotta do is play the game and shit will start fallin' your way."

"If you say so," she said, glancing at her phone. "I'd love to chat more, guys, but it's a bit past my bedtime and I'd like to get a few hours of shuteye before the sun comes up."

Daniel checked his phone: 3:14 a.m.

"Fine," he said. "You can take the guest room. I'll get you fresh sheets if you need them. I'll be in my room, so holler if you need anything. Andre, my guy, I'm sorry, but you're on the couch."

"Man, ain't this some shit." Andre walked away from the table in a huff. He threw himself on the couch and kicked his shoes off. "Guess if I can sleep in that cramped-ass car, I can sleep here."

Sarah removed her hair band and rustled her brown locks loose. Daniel placed a hand on her arm, and she flinched again.

"Thank you for your help on this," Daniel said. "We're glad to have you, and we know this is high-risk business."

She stared at him behind tired eyes, which closed as her cheeks rose with a smile.

"No prob," she said, getting up from her seat and strolling to the stairs. "Night, boys."

Daniel watched her leave. Andre was already snoring on the couch; that guy fell asleep faster than anybody Daniel knew. With the way Daniel had been struggling to sleep lately, he was jealous. After Sarah's footsteps came to a stop and the door to the guest room closed, he headed for his own room.

Clothes were scattered all over the floor by his dresser. Was this his doing, or did Sarah leave his room a mess while looking for a shirt and shorts to steal from him? The closet was open, too, but nothing appeared out of place. He walked over and shut the closet before picking up and folding all the scattered clothes, gently putting them back in the drawers. There were some items in there he hadn't worn in years and others that brought back immediate memories of Gabby: trips with her to exotic locales, jobs across the country with Andre when they needed to get out of the city, drunken late-night online shopping binges. Some of it made him smile, the rest made him cringe as he remembered their last fight.

Once everything was in order, Daniel pulled a phone charger out of the drawer and plugged it in before connecting it to his phone. It was at one percent.

The sheets on his bed were still messed up from the last time he rushed out of here. He shook the dust off, disrobed, and fell into bed. Daniel grabbed another pillow to cuddle and pressed it against his chest, squeezing tight, refusing to let it out of his grasp.

5

SOARING EAGLE JERKED AWAKE AND found himself
covered in sweat. He clutched the sides of his mattress
and sat up, searching around the room for the beast that
had inhabited his nightmare. The lingering sound of fingernails
scratching along the walls was imprinted in his mind. Reality
was silent, save for the birds chirping outside. The sun peeked
over the horizon out his window, and cool desert air made its
way into his room. He lifted himself out of bed and slipped on a
pair of moccasins before heading outside.

Wind washed over his dark, wrinkled skin. Braids hung to
his chest, and his old bones ached. Over the Paiute reservation,
dust kicked up in the beams of sunlight as he took deep breaths
in and out. He groaned while lowering himself to his cabin's
front steps. Horse hooves clopped at an increasing volume until
his daughter came into sight. Right on time.

The legs and underside of the white stallion were caked with
dirt, and Soaring Eagle thought Jennifer ought to take better care
of her horse. But now was not the time to scold her: an important
message needed to be delivered to the rest of the tribe, and she
was the quickest method of delivery. As the tribe's only medical

doctor, they trusted Jennifer and valued her words. The horse slowed as it approached the edge of the porch.

"Good morning, Dad," Jennifer said. Her wide face flashed a smile beneath the brim of her cowboy hat. Her small nose reminded Soaring Eagle of his late wife. "Do you need anything from the store today? I'll be headed that way this morning."

"No. Thank you, sweetheart. Hitch your horse and come inside. I have an important message for our people."

Jennifer furrowed her brow. She hopped off her horse, hitched it to a post, and followed her father inside. The pair sat across from each other at the dining room table. Photos of Jennifer as a young child were stuck to the fridge with magnets. She smiled as she observed them, and her father reached out to grab her hands.

"I had a troubling dream last night—one of darkness and pain. I worry it portends danger for us, and for our neighbors to the South."

Jennifer paused to process her father's words.

"What do you mean? What did you see?"

"Blood flowing through Las Vegas in a river. A powerful man corrupted by greed and lust. His mind did not belong to him. And…"

Jennifer leaned closer.

"And?" she asked, concern on her face.

"A Wendigo," Soaring Eagle said, the image from his dream returning to his mind: a dark figure with yellow eyes lurking in the shadows, its claws scraping on the walls and leaving burn marks in their wake. Soaring Eagle was relieved that his daughter appeared to believe him, as many young people in the tribe had lost interest in the old traditions and viewed his dreams and visions as superstition. But what he felt last night and into this morning was unmistakable.

"Are you sure?" Jennifer asked.

"Yes, though I haven't dealt with one in my lifetime. It has taken hold of someone in the city, that much I know. It is not yet clear to me who is in its grasp, but we have to warn our leaders."

"What should I tell them?"

"Tell them I need to speak with them at length about an imminent threat; that I need a moment of their time at the next council meeting."

Jennifer nodded and headed for the door. She stopped herself before grabbing the doorknob and turning back.

"Are you sure you don't need anything from the store?"

Soaring Eagle smiled. He was proud to have raised such a caring young woman; a doctor who did far more for her community than treat their ailments. She was the glue that held the tribe together through her words and actions.

"I could use some milk. Thanks."

Jennifer left. Soaring Eagle buried his face in his hands and massaged his forehead with the tips of his fingers. He returned to his bedroom and thumbed through the bookshelf, finding the oldest and most weathered book he owned. He sat at his desk and flipped the yellowing pages to a section near the book's center. The words of his ancestors bounced around in his mind until they formed a coherent narrative.

A Wendigo can take many forms. It can masquerade as a human-like entity or possess a vulnerable host. Its insatiable hunger for human flesh drives men to madness. Whatever the man desires—be it pleasure of the flesh or power or wealth—the Wendigo corrupts his mind into thinking it is attainable through nefarious means.

Soaring Eagle paused to examine an artist's rendering of the creature in its true form. He considered painting what he saw in his dream, and this book would be a good guide. The depiction gave him chills. Over a black background, a horned beast emerged from the shadows, with red skin and long, bony limbs that extended down to abnormally large hands. Its fingernails were black and sharpened at the ends. Its face was triangular with gnashing teeth surrounded by cracked, black lips. A forked tongue came out of its angry maw, and its eyes were crying blood. Soaring Eagle felt the Wendigo staring at him from the page. He shuddered and flipped to the next one.

The Wendigo was first seen in the east by the Cree people and traveled west, bringing disease, famine, and agony with it. It found itself attached to the White man, encouraging him to inflict horrors upon our people and other tribes throughout the continent. Its destruction lasted for decades; its effects on our daily lives are still felt to this day. There is no clear method for killing a Wendigo, although it can be weakened through a ghost dance or acts of sacrifice. Be wary of the offers it makes, because a Wendigo's strength is derived from corruption and control.

Soaring Eagle shut the book. He placed it back on the shelf and returned to his bed, resting his eyes as lay on his back with his hands folded across his chest. He meditated on the words he read, thinking of whom in the city might be under this spirit's control. Wind carried the leftover smell of rain. A scratching noise echoed in the room again.

Soaring Eagle opened his eyes: nothing in his immediate view. But as he leaned back, a book flew off the shelf and landed face down on the floor. He shot up, staring in awe and fear. Taking measured steps toward the book, he realized it was the same one he had just been reading. He leaned over and picked it up hesitantly.

When Soaring Eagle turned it over, the book was open to the drawing of the Wendigo. In lieu of the scowl he had observed on the beast's face before, it was now smiling wide, lips curled up and teeth pressed together. Soaring Eagle tossed the book across the room, and it shut as it hit the ground.

Bewildered and breathing heavily, Soaring Eagle decided to get dressed and leave home for the time being. As he walked out the door, he grabbed a black cowboy hat with assorted feathers emblazoned on the front and put it on. He slammed the door shut behind him and began his walk. As the sun made its way above him, it warmed the back of his neck. The further he got from his home, the safer he felt. Red rocks towered above the valley and provided shade as he approached. A path in the side of the rock, carved out centuries ago, led him to the top, and he struggled through the steeper portions of the hike. *Aging is a natural process but a frustrating one.*

Soaring Eagle sat cross-legged on a smoothed-out ledge, a once sprawling natural view now partially obscured by the faraway city. Even in the day and from a considerable distance, the flashing lights of Las Vegas reflected in his eyes; a monument to the White man's greed, but a revenue stream for many of his people, all the same. He had learned to accept the rapid changes coming to the land his great-grandfather had hunted. *Land—like the animals and people inhabiting it—inevitably dies and becomes something else*, he thought. Soaring Eagle took in a deep breath through his nose and out through his mouth. His throat felt dry. A sip of water from his canteen provided a brief remedy.

Finally, peace. His eyes could close without worrying about whatever was haunting him. Was it the Wendigo playing tricks? Did it anticipate Soaring Eagle's role in the war to come? They were notoriously insightful creatures, capable of things men could only dream of. *And it is the dreams and aspirations of men*, Soaring Eagle thought, *that must have drawn it to this place: a city of sins, and what better place to take advantage of man's short-term desires?*

He had partaken in gambling before. And drinking. And—

much to the dismay of Jennifer's late mother—philandering. But that was many years ago, when he was young and arrogant, when he attributed his uncanny visions to being a "chosen one," destined to lead his people out of squalor. But that was a folly of pride. His wife's suicide changed him. The pain Soaring Eagle caused that he believed had led to her death was too much even for his ego to bear. He would spend hours out here, crying, gazing upward for answers, only to find them by looking inward.

Soaring Eagle considered himself lucky that his daughter was too young to understand the events leading to her mother's death. It was a story that got closer to reality as Jennifer got older but never close enough to reveal the full picture. Her image of her father was one on a pedestal, and when he stepped down from it and shuttered himself in that distant country home, Jennifer cared for him like she cared for so many in her adult life. Soaring Eagle resisted her help at first, but like many of his great changes, he put pride aside and allowed others into his emotional and physical space.

Soaring Eagle opened his eyes and felt the heat he was baking under. Many hours of meditation had stretched into the afternoon, and the sun was too high for him to be out here much longer. He took careful steps back down the rock and made the journey home. When he returned, Jennifer was sitting on the porch, waiting for him with a liter of milk.

The moment reminded Soaring Eagle of when his daughter was young, when he'd come home from a night of work to find Jennifer sitting in a similar position, eagerly anticipating the hot meal her dad would cook up for the night. They were luckier than most: a sprawling ranch with plenty of money flowing in from the tribe's casino ventures. Were they less fortunate, Jennifer could have easily turned to drinking or drugs and found herself in the pit so many in her generation were incapable of climbing out of. But she was a married doctor with a child. What more could a father ask for?

Soaring Eagle reached out and patted Jennifer on the shoulder.

"What did the council say?"

"They said you can address your concerns at the next meeting in a few days."

"And did they seem receptive of the message? Are they interested in learning more?"

"They…" she hesitated. "They were skeptical, Dad. You know how it is. It's a new council; some of them just don't understand. It took some convincing before they agreed to hear you out."

"Hmm… I see. Then it will take more than just a story to convince them to take action. What that looks like, I do not know. What I do know is that you are likely hungry, my sweet girl. Have you eaten yet?"

Jennifer shrugged her shoulders. "Not yet. Been a busy day."

Soaring Eagle grinned. He hadn't cooked for her in a while. "Do you want Three Sisters soup?"

"Oh my gosh," she said, holding her stomach. "That sounds incredible."

Soaring Eagle's smile grew. "I believe I have the ingredients, so let's get to it. Start chopping the onion I have on the counter, and I'll gather the rest of what we need."

Jennifer nodded and headed inside. As Soaring Eagle entered the front door, he turned back to the mountains at the edge of the valley. Dark rain clouds were forming in the distance. Another storm was on its way.

6

"**C**AN YOU ZIP ME UP?" Sarah asked, her arms twisting to reach the center of her back. She wanted to do it herself, but the dress was too tight. Daniel came to the rescue and helped her finish with a quick zip. She looked herself up and down in the mirror and caught him doing the same.

"Like what you see?" she asked.

"Uhh… y-yeah," Daniel stammered. "The blue dress and matching eyeshadow really make your eyes pop. Reynolds won't know what hit him."

Sarah wished he'd wrap his arms around her waist and hug her from behind, but he seemed hesitant. She'd taken a liking to him in the time they'd spent together, and she needed the reassurance right now. Despite the confidence she often displayed in front of Daniel and Andre, her anxiety was starting to build for the night ahead. She had rehearsed some of her go-to lines ahead of time; the rest would be improvised. *Has to feel natural. Have to make him think you're worth it.*

"Let's knock this bastard dead," Sarah said, lifting her fists in the mirror. Daniel shot her a half-concerned glance. "But not literally, of course."

"That's the spirit," he said.

They walked arm in arm down the wide staircase to a waiting Andre, who was loading bullets into the chamber of his gun. She wondered if Daniel had done the same and if they would need to use them. She brought protection of her own as well, but it's always nice to have guns at your back if a situation goes south.

"Sweet… baby… Jesus," Andre said, checking her out. "You lookin' fine as hell tonight, mama. I might have to take you out to dinner and say fuck all this schemin' shit. How's steak and lobster sound?"

Sarah smiled through pink lipstick.

"I might just take you up on that."

Andre raised an eyebrow and opened the front door for her. Daniel followed, and she could hear them jockeying with each other behind her. What was she getting into with these guys? Two doofuses trying to pull off the heist of a lifetime.

Daniel hurried ahead and opened the car door for her. She lowered herself in carefully while Andre hopped in the back with her. Daniel took the wheel and turned back to them.

"You know, Andre, they don't make you guys sit in the back anymore. You don't have to do it every time."

"Man, fuck you. I'll sit where I like. There's more room back here, anyway, and she's a lot better to look at than your bum ass. Smells better, too."

Daniel's shoulders shook with laughter as he turned the keys. The car clicked but wouldn't start.

"Fuck," Daniel said, slapping the steering wheel. He tried to start it again to no avail.

He shrugged his shoulders to his passengers. Sarah glared at him.

"Are you fucking kidding me?" she said.

"Looks like we're gonna have to hail a cab. Andre, can you

call your buddy at the taxi service and tell him it's a 'special delivery?'"

Andre sighed and pulled out his phone. After some extended negotiation, they had a ride. It was ten minutes away. They stood on the sidewalk by the parked car while Daniel smoked a cigarette. Sarah's mind raced as she gazed up at the stars. The first thing—the first fucking thing—already went wrong. What would be next? Would the bouncer not let her in? Did Reynolds already know they were coming? How could they trust the guys at this taxi company?

The car pulled up. Sarah swung the door open and got in the back. Andre knocked Daniel out of the way and sat shotgun, leaving him in the back with Sarah. She liked it better that way, sweet as Andre was. She felt a different kind of safe with Daniel. Her nerves started to calm.

Andre and the cabbie went on about the prospect of a professional basketball team coming to Las Vegas. Sarah tuned most of it out. As they got closer to the hotel across from The Luxury, where Daniel and Andre would be listening in and ready to intervene, Sarah gripped Daniel's hand tightly. He flinched at first, but then placed his other hand on top of hers and gave her a reassuring glance. She decided right then that she would sleep with him when the night was over. With all the adrenaline she'd have built up, he was in for a wild ride.

The trio got out of the taxi and stood in the parking garage, Sarah across from Daniel with Andre looking on.

"Welp, guess this is where we split," Sarah said. "You guys all set across the way?"

"Yep," Daniel replied, gesturing to his ear. "We'll be in your ear the whole time. This thing is strong enough to hear what's around you, too, so if we pick up anything fishy, we'll let you know."

Sarah nodded in approval. She took a second to get her bearings then made an impulse decision to run to Daniel and hug him. His arms remained wide for a second before he squeezed her tightly.

"You'll be great," he said. "Don't sweat it."

She could see fear on his face. It made her feel better, for whatever reason, that he was scared too. It didn't feel crazy to suddenly drop her guard and hug him like that. They separated, and she went on her way, high heels tapping on the concrete the whole way to Reynolds's hotel. The building loomed at an imposing height above Sarah, as if it was leaning forward. She pushed herself through the revolving door and strutted through row after row of slot machines. A few men gawked at her when she strolled by, but she was otherwise inconspicuous, blending into a city full of women like her playing far less dangerous games. She thought about stopping at the bar for a drink first—for courage—but didn't want to be late.

In the darkest corner of the sportsbook, a massive gentleman in an all-black suit with a white bowtie stood with his arms crossed. He was her barrier to entry. She took lazy steps, hips swinging, up to the bruiser and gave a cute wave as she approached and handed him her ID.

"Hey there, big guy. I'm here for the card game. Name is Sarah Wallace."

He checked her driver's license, then her face.

"You look different."

"Oh, yeah. That's 'cause I changed my hair. Used to be blonde, but you know what they say: Brunettes have more fun!"

The security guard snickered before handing her back the license. He waved her through. She reached up and pecked him on the cheek. The hallway back to the table was dark with the exception of one fluorescent lightbulb swinging above her. On the right, down another dark stretch of hallway, the only door in sight was cracked open to reveal a room with the lights on. She made her way inside and walked into a cloud of cigar smoke. Two nights in a row, she was reminded of her dad's nasty habit. But she stopped herself from scrunching her nose to the smell and sat with a casual flair in her seat. Reynolds wasn't there yet.

She examined the band of thugs sitting in a semicircle around the extra-large table. The dealer was on her phone and didn't acknowledge Sarah's presence. The rest of the crowd was stuffy rich assholes in expensive suits, along with a couple biker types who seemed out of place. Sarah figured they probably had some cash to burn from whatever drug trade they found themselves entangled in. She tried to ignore one with a ZZ Top beard who appeared to be ogling her breasts from across the room.

Heavy footsteps filled the hallway, and the conversation in the room hushed. The sound of a cane between each step clacked and echoed into the room. Around the corner, Reynolds slithered in, sunken eyes hiding behind sunglasses that he definitely didn't need indoors. He wore a dark, sharkskin suit and leather shoes that shined in the light. His wrinkled hands sported several expensive rings. On any other night, Sarah would have tried to find a way to lift them. Maybe she'd take one for the road if he got drunk enough later.

"You faggots ready to play?" he grumbled. Everyone forced laughter in the room except for her. She caught his eye, and he seemed surprised to see her. "Well, excuse me, miss. Didn't mean to speak such vulgarities in front of a lady. Your name, darling?"

"Sarah," she said, extending a hand. He kissed it with dry, crusted lips. "Sarah Wallace."

He didn't seem suspicious of her. He seemed captivated and just as horny as Andre had described him.

"Well, however you found yourself at one of my card games, Ms. Wallace, it's nice to have a beautiful woman in here for a change. These games were getting to be a sausage fest. Forgive us if we get a bit too rambunctious. This is a competitive bunch of cavemen, you see."

"No problem at all," she said through a forced smile. "I've got a bit of fire in me, too."

He turned his head at an angle and raised his eyebrow. She ran a hand across his sleeve. He grunted as he sat in a higher chair than his competition. *Even in something as small as blackjack*, she thought, *he has to be on some kind of throne.*

The game got rolling, and the hours passed with an increasing collection of empty beer bottles at Reynolds's feet. He didn't even bother to set them there, just tossed them for someone else to clean up. Sarah had a few drinks herself, but not enough to knock her off her game. It would take a lot to do that. She knew her way around a bottle, one thing she had her dad's genes to thank for.

As her chips began to pile up and some of the crowd cleared out, Reynolds lifted himself up and whispered in her ear.

"Wanna head up to my place for a nightcap?"

The game was far from finished. Reynolds was still in a good spot with his chips, and the plan was to finish the game with him cleared out before going upstairs. He needed to be drunk enough to spill the beans. Was he?

She hesitated. "Sure. Let me just freshen up in the little girls' room."

"Fine by me, sweetheart," he croaked. "My bathroom is out of commission, anyway. Issue with my shower."

She nodded and made her way to the women's restroom down the hall. She got inside, locked the door, and turned on the listening device in her ear.

"Daniel, Andre, can you hear me?"

She heard rustling and whispers as they picked up on the other end—Daniel and Andre probably weren't expecting to hear from her so early.

"Yeah, we can hear you," Daniel said across the airwaves. His voice calmed her again. "What's up?"

"Card game's over. We're heading up to his room now."

"Shit, okay. Is he drunk enough to be taken advantage of?"

"As much as he's going to be, I guess. I'll try and pour a few more in him."

"Okay. Try and keep us updated. And be careful."

She paused, wondering if it she'd be able to execute their plan given the change of circumstances. At this point, she had no choice. She washed her hands and checked herself out in the bathroom mirror: not a wrinkle in the dress as it clung to her figure. She felt confident, sexy, ready to peel secrets out of this dirtbag.

She hurried out of the bathroom and found him standing there, waiting. He extended an arm and guided her through the halls and out toward the elevator. On their way, casino employees nodded and smiled in his direction. He ignored them. After a while, it felt like *she* was guiding *him*—he felt old, tired, as if a lowkey night of drinking and gambling wore him out. They arrived at his private elevator, and he whipped out a key. The elevator dinged, but the light didn't come on. *Weird*. Still, the door slid open, and they slipped inside.

He tried to kiss her on the neck on the way up. She relented a bit and smiled.

"Hold off there, tiger. We've got a lot more talking and drinking to do before we get to the touching."

He seemed thrown off, but he smiled and bowed to her.

"Anyth-thing for you, my queen," he slurred. He was more fucked up than she thought.

Another ding. They made it to the penthouse. Marble floors led to luxurious furniture, and romantic music playing on the speakers. A single red rose in a vase sat on his coffee table alongside chocolate-covered strawberries. No doubt he had told one of his minions to get this all set up. She had to stop herself from gagging at the romanticism.

"Whaddaya think?" he asked, turning to her with his eyes swimming in drunken satisfaction. He appeared younger, happier, as if something gave him back the life force that had been drained from years in Vegas's underbelly. *Is it the booze, or something else?*

"Looks great, honey," Sarah said. "What can I get for ya to drink?"

He placed a hand on her butt and squeezed. "You're a real doll. Gin and tonic, *por favor*."

She removed his hand from her backside and watched him stumble over to the couch, cane dragging on the floor. He fell into the seat and leaned his head back, laughing like he was surprised he made it. His eyes closed as the laughter slowed down. His mouth remained open. He took long, heavy breaths.

She turned her back on him to pour the drinks. Gin and tonic for him, soda water for her. She even put a tiny umbrella in her drink to sell the con. When she turned around, Reynolds was standing right behind her, dumb smile on his face. It made her jump and nearly spill the contents of the glasses. She handed him his stiff one.

"Jesus, Richard. You scared me half to death."

He paused and stared off into the distance.

"'Half to death,'" he repeated before locking eyes with her. "My ex-wife used to say that. I think it's fuckin' stupid. You're either dead or alive, sweetheart, and one of us is closer to the former."

She faked a sweet laugh and put a gentle hand on his chest.

"Oh, Richard. You've got plenty of exciting years ahead of ya. Don't get morbid now."

Reynolds shrugged his shoulders and let out a half-hearted chuckle.

"I guess."

Sarah led him back to the couch. He seemed despondent and set his drink down. She put it back in his hand and held up her glass.

"To us," she said, pecking him on the cheek. He perked up from his drunken stupor.

"To you, my dear. And to the future!"

Their glasses clinked. They each took hearty sips. He set his down and leaned back again. She put down her own and placed a hand on his leg, rubbing it slowly.

"So, how's work been?" she asked.

"Ehh, issalright. Could be—" he belched, "better."

"Why's that?" She moved her hand toward his inseam.

"I'm jusfuckin' tired. I'm gettin' old, Sarah. This game iss-gettin' too fast for the old boy. Ha!"

He laughed and stared down the hallway, smiling behind an empty gaze.

"I keep sayin' that shit: 'old boy.' Thassafuckin' oxymoron, ain't it?"

She was confused about what he was looking at. She laughed anyway.

"Yes, baby. Sure is. So, what do you mean that things are 'getting too fast?'"

Reynolds grabbed his glass with surprising speed and hurled it down the hallway. It shattered on impact, and he stood up, pointing in anger. Sarah was startled but calmed herself.

"F-f-fuck you!" he spat before falling back into his seat.

"Aww, Richard. Let me clean that up for you."

He didn't reply. He was leaning way back again, facing up toward the ceiling—only this time, his eyes were wide open. His breathing was heavier. She worried he might be having a heart attack, the old bastard, but she ignored it and headed to his kitchen. She grabbed a towel, dustpan, and hand broom from under the sink and headed down the hallway, still playing the part. It was dark except for a light on in the bathroom. *Didn't he say it was getting worked on?*

Sarah found the glass scattered just short of the bathroom door, forming a misshapen triangle of shards with a puddle of booze underneath. She knelt down and sopped up the liquid with the towel, carefully avoiding pieces of glass, and got to work sweeping. Her eyes searched for every speck, sweeping it into the pan with meticulous detail. She slid on her knees closer to the bathroom door, and the light went out. She heard breathing and thought Reynolds had come stumbling over to help, but the sound hadn't come from behind her.

Sarah froze. Standing down the hall from her was a towering black figure with long arms and massive hands. Its sunken chest rose and fell with increasing speed. Its yellow, cat-like eyes glowed as it flashed its teeth. A rotten smell made her eyes water. Out of instinct, she pulled her pistol from the holster strapped to her thigh.

The beast jerked forward, taking three massive steps toward her as she cocked the gun. Sarah lifted her arm, and a jagged black fingernail flashed in front of her. Sharp pain cut across her throat as she dropped the gun.

Sarah reached for her neck. Hot blood poured through her fingers. She gargled and crumpled to the floor with a thud. Everything was silent for a moment, pain reverberating throughout her neck and chest. Through the quiet, she began to hear breathing above her and slow footsteps behind her, the intermittent tap of a cane between them. Her eyes rolled back in her head leaving nothing but darkness.

7

ANDRE TWIDDLED HIS THUMBS AND ground his teeth with nervous repetition. He looked up from his hands to Daniel, who lay on the bed with his eyes closed and arms wide. Their hotel room had a view of The Luxury across the street, but Reynolds's balcony was too high up to keep a watchful eye on Sarah. Andre spotted a Hispanic woman in lingerie gazing out the window of a room level with theirs. Through his binoculars, which otherwise went unused, he observed her full breasts, wide hips, and dark hair up in a bun. A fat old man emerged from the shadows behind her, hair running down his pale belly. He straddled her from behind and kissed her neck. Andre shuddered, tossing the binoculars aside.

Through the speaker, as if on cue, glass shattered in Reynolds's room. Daniel leapt out of bed, and Andre jumped in his seat. Andre ran over to the surveillance equipment and turned up the volume as Daniel huddled next to him.

"F-f-fuck you!" Reynolds yelled. Was Sarah in trouble? Had she pissed him off?

"Aww, Richard. Let me clean that up for you," she said. She was okay, Andre thought, and still playing her role. Reynolds must have just popped off and broken something.

Andre listened as Sarah's high heels tapped on the marble floors, and he heard her sweeping up glass. What a mess Reynolds must have been.

Silence.

Andre watched Daniel shrug his shoulders. They both jumped when three loud thumps came over the speakers. Then a slice followed by gurgling. A head hit the floor.

Andre grabbed the radio.

"Yo, Sarah, you alright?"

Nothing.

"Sarah, let us know if you're alright, girl. Come on now."

Heavy breathing came through the receiver. Reynolds's steps and cane taps were audible in the background. Daniel reached for the device and shut it off with haste.

"Dan, man, the fuck you doin'? We gotta make sure she's alright!"

Daniel was pale, gaunt, staring at Andre behind glassy eyes. Something was wrong, and Andre could tell his friend had a gut feeling of what went down.

"We have to get over there," Daniel said.

"Bro, how? There's no way up to that room other than the one elevator."

Daniel's eyes darted around the room.

"Then we get the security footage, figure out what happened."

"That's a tall task, my guy. Reynolds has an armed guard outside that shit, and we didn't plan on doin' any killing tonight—"

"Fuck our plans! Sarah is in danger right now. Do you even fucking care? Get off your ass, get your gun, and let's go."

Andre threw up his arms and walked over to his bag. He pulled out his pistol and silencer, twisting them together. He watched Daniel do the same but at a far more frenetic pace. Daniel led the way as they stuck the weapons in their concealed holsters and marched out of the hotel room. Striding through the lobby and out the front doors of their hotel, rain pounded on the duo as they crossed the street. Andre kept an eye out for cars, but Daniel's focus remained straight ahead the whole time.

"Yo, Dan, slow the hell down," Andre said through the storm. It was raining hard—large drops coming down fast. Andre didn't bother protecting his hair. Daniel smacked the revolving door open, and Andre scooted through behind him. Everything seemed so *normal* in the casino hall. Slot machines rang, people chatted, and smoke filled the air: a typical night for everybody but them. Andre wondered if everyone was watching them—especially Daniel who was speed walking like a bat out of hell.

Having previously scouted out the entire building, they headed for the sports book and followed a dark hallway into the bowels of the casino. Andre ran through the main floor's layout in his head, thinking about dark corners that hostiles might be lurking in, and how he and Daniel were in a blind spot for the security cameras. Outside a room with a door that had a fingerprint scanner on its handle, a massive figure in a black suit stood with his arms crossed. He spotted Daniel and reached for his sidearm, but Andre watched Daniel whip out his gun and fire two silent rounds into the guy's face, one in the forehead and another just below his nose. Blood splattered on his white bowtie. He collapsed to the floor with a soft thud, and Daniel pointed his gun at the door handle.

"Whoa, whoa, Dan. Wait!"

Daniel had anger and impatience in his eyes.

"Fucking what, Andre?"

Andre crept over to the security guard's corpse and lifted up a heavy arm. He got ready to press the limp thumb to the scanner and turned to Daniel.

"Soon as I do this, bust that door open and cap whoever's in there."

Daniel nodded, drawing quick circles in the air with his finger to indicate Andre should hurry up. Andre pressed the guard's fat thumb on the scanner and the light went green. Daniel lowered his shoulder on the door as he turned the handle, and Andre watched as he sent two bullets zinging into the back of two men's heads before they could even turn around.

Daniel ran to the right and tossed a corpse out of the way before sitting in his chair. Andre went left and scooted the chair out of the way, the henchman's body still slumped over in it. His bloody skull dragged along the control board, and Andre gagged before taking a knee.

Daniel fiddled with the controls until he pulled up tape of Reynolds's room. They both examined the biggest screen at the center of the monitors and saw Reynolds standing over Sarah. She lay in a pool of blood around her upper body. Daniel screamed and punched one of the secondary monitors, shattering it in the process. Blood dripped from the shards of glass in his fist. Andre reached out to try and calm him down.

"Dan, Dan, relax. Ain't nothing we can do for her now. We've got to get the fuck up outta here."

Andre hated seeming emotionless, having to be the voice of reason for Daniel in this moment of agony. He could tell his best friend was catching feelings for that girl. Even if he wasn't, this was a fucking tragedy. The job was beyond being in jeopardy; it had gone full bust.

Daniel slapped Andre's hand away and stared at him, tears now welling up in his eyes. His hair was wet from the rain and hanging in front of his face.

"I'm not fuckin' leaving. Not yet."

Daniel reached for the controls and rewound the tape. He got to a point where Sarah was on her knees, cleaning the glass. *Nothing out of the ordinary*, Andre thought. They watched as Sarah stopped cleaning and froze, staring into the dark hallway. There was no noise on the tape, but out of nowhere, she reached for her gun then dropped it. She put both hands up to her throat and fell as blood began to pool around her. Nobody was there to slit her throat. She twitched on the ground before falling limp. Reynolds strolled into the frame, cane in hand. He tossed it aside and walked toward her body without favoring his bad leg. Squatting down, he ran his finger through the pool of blood. When he put the finger to his tongue, the tape cut out.

Daniel didn't speak. Andre couldn't either for a second, until he grabbed Daniel by the shoulder.

"Dan, we gotta get out of here."

Daniel stared at Andre with an empty gaze. He stood up and headed for the door, ripping it open before firing a few more rounds into the security guard's corpse. He pulled another cartridge of bullets from the inside of his jacket and reloaded. Andre ran over and stopped him from wasting them on the stiff.

"Dan, bro, relax. Let's go."

But that's when Andre saw it: a keyring hanging from the belt of the deceased, blood from his bullet-riddled belly pouring onto it. *Could one of those be the key to Reynolds's elevator?* Daniel must have thought the same thing because he grabbed the keyring and ran down the hallway. Andre followed, as he had done all night. He was getting sick of chasing this dude, and now Daniel had really lost it: he actually thought he could get up to Reynolds's place without issue.

Daniel bobbed and weaved around gamblers and families with small children, Andre trailing close behind and apologizing to the people he knocked around. They arrived at the elevator and Daniel fiddled with the keys, blood streaking on his hands. He jammed two different keys in the slot to no avail before trying a third. It worked. With everything that had gone wrong tonight, maybe their luck was turning.

"Let's go," Daniel said. They hopped in the elevator and pressed *Up*. The car was filled with a rotten stench as it ascended.

As the elevator approached Reynolds's room, Andre drew his gun. Daniel already had his raised. With a pair of dings, the doors slid open. The lights were off in the room and it was silent—nobody on the couch at the center of the room, nobody in the kitchen on the right. Andre checked the hallway past the kitchen and made his way to the area where Sarah had been killed. He walked step for step with Daniel over to the scene of the crime. No corpse, no blood on the floor, no broken glass, no scuffs on the pristine marble—it didn't make sense. This had happened within the last half hour. *No way Reynolds could have sent his goons to clean it up that fast.* He peeked at Daniel who appeared confused as he searched around the empty hallway.

"Dan…"

He put up a hand to quiet Andre, keeping his gun raised. Andre followed him to Reynolds's bedroom. Daniel tried the knob, but it was locked. He kicked the door in and found more darkness. No lights on, nobody in there. The bed was made neatly, like when someone arrives at a hotel. No evidence of anybody having been there in days let alone minutes or hours. Andre walked back out into the hallway and checked the bathroom. The lights wouldn't turn on, and nobody was hiding in the busted-up shower or anywhere else.

Ding. Ding.

The elevator was opening on the other side of the suite. Andre heard it and signaled to Daniel to take cover. He pressed up against the bathroom door and peeked around the corner while Daniel did the same in the bedroom doorway. Five thugs armed with assault rifles lumbered into view. Reynolds wasn't among them. The one in front signaled to three of them to head down the hallway while he and the other one investigated the living room.

They were wearing bulletproof vests, and their heads were exposed. Andre knew the odds were long, considering there were three of them coming down the hall, and out of the corner of his eye, he saw Daniel waving from the other doorway. Daniel counted down on his fingers. Three… Two… One…

Andre and Daniel fired two rounds at the thugs in quick succession. One struck the first in line in the head, toppling him to the ground, while another whizzed past the second in line. Andre fired two more before the rain of bullets came hurtling down the hallway. Daniel fired another and Andre heard the rattle of just one assault rifle in response. There would surely be two more coming soon. Andre's hands were moist and shaking on his pistol when he saw the bullets were flying toward Daniel's doorway. This was his shot. He leaned out the doorway and fired three rounds at the gunman, two striking his head and another sailing above him as he fell. Rounds scattered in random directions from his AR-15 as the man collapsed, and a bullet struck Andre in the shoulder. Stinging pain radiated down his arm. He grimaced and slid back behind the doorway.

Two men were running—the last two. Andre was ready to turn and fire when he stopped himself. Daniel was walking down the hallway with his hands up, gun holstered. *What the fuck are you doing?* Andre wanted to whisper at Daniel, but he figured it out: he was giving himself up so Andre could escape. *But why?* Andre made quick, quiet movements toward the shower.

"Fellas, you got me," Daniel said. A pistol whipped across Daniel's skull. Andre had heard that sound plenty of times before, but it never gave him pause until this moment. Daniel hit the floor, and Andre stepped around broken glass into the deep bathtub. He went out of his way not to make a sound as he lowered himself into the basin. No broken glass cracked, nothing slipped or jingled against the ceramic surface.

Andre heard one of the men step into the bathroom. When his steps sounded like they were heading back out the door, Andre peeked his eyes up over the edge of the tub and saw him investigating the blood smear on the door. It was from his shoulder, which Andre just now realized was hurting like a motherfucker. Would this guy figure out that Daniel wasn't alone? Andre watched him search the hallway one direction then the other before leaving without further investigation. He let out a silent breath of relief and leaned back into the tub.

The elevator dinged and Andre assumed the thugs were leaving with Daniel in tow, but he heard a raspy voice echo throughout the room.

"Looks like you guys got me a present," Reynolds croaked.

"He killed three of our guys before we got to him."

There was a pause for what Andre assumed to be Reynolds's inspection of the corpses.

"Well, all is fair in love and war, gentlemen. Let's get our buddy Daniel to the warehouse and call it a night. No way I'm sleeping in here with all those bodies. Oleg, book me a room at Caesar's and send the cleanup crew in here again."

How does he know Dan's name?

Andre waited for a few minutes after the group entered the elevator. He lifted himself out of the tub and took measured steps to avoid alerting anyone who might be left over. But once he got to the hallway, he realized it was just him and the dead. He stepped over their bodies and made it to the elevator. Andre pressed *Down*, and the car arrived—empty—for him to take a ride down. The rancid odor from before was even stronger now.

Andre leaned against the railing in the elevator and put his face in his hands. It stung his shoulder to lift the arm, but he didn't care. The elevator arrived at the ground floor. Andre's eyes widened as the door slid open and two hotel staff members were staring back at him. They wore hazmat suits stood in front of a cart of cleaning materials and body bags. They seemed surprised to see him.

"Get up there and clean that shit up," Andre ordered them,

pretending to be one of Reynolds's men. "And gimme a fuckin' towel."

Andre grabbed a large towel and folded it longways, draping it over his bloody shoulder like he was on his way to the pool. It did the trick and blood didn't soak through—yet. He walked casually through the casino and out the front door. Surely, Andre thought, he'd be picked up by the security cameras, but by the time Reynolds realized what had happened he'd already be way out of town. Rain still fell hard outside as Andre trudged across the street, arriving at his Mercedes in the parking garage. It was all fixed up by Gus and waiting with the keys in the glove box in case he and Daniel needed a fast escape. Now it was just him, and who knows where they were taking Daniel.

"I'll come back for you, brotha," Andre said under his breath as he gripped the car door. He got in and popped open the glove box before starting up the engine. Andre whipped the steering wheel with his good arm and peeled out of the parking garage, heading north up Las Vegas Boulevard to the only doctor he could see who wouldn't ask questions.

8

S HE WAS STANDING IN THE doorway, red dress clinging
to her curves. Her hazel eyes bid him to come closer. Daniel obliged as he wrapped Sarah in his arms and carried
her to the bed. He fell on top of her. They both laughed, kissed
and groped at each other's clothes. Daniel ran his hands down
the side of her face and to her neck. It was warm. He opened
his eyes to find blood on his fingers. He pulled away and saw
that her face was pale, frozen in fear, eyes wide. Her throat was
slashed open. Blood spilled all over the white linens around her.

"Why…" she coughed up, "didn't you save me?"

"I… I'm sorry. I'm so sorry," Daniel said, backing away
from the bed.

Sarah sat up and twisted her head in his direction. Her eyes
were gone, replaced by oozing sockets. Her throat continued to
gush. She pointed at him and screamed.

"This is *your* fault! *YOU* did this!"

Daniel fell through the floor and jerked awake. He was in a
warehouse, sitting in a chair, his hands tied behind his back. He
peered through swollen eyes at the dark expanse of the building,
a spotlight above him the only thing he could see with complete

clarity. His forehead throbbed, and dried blood crusted below his nostrils. His mouth tasted like metal.

"Hello?" Daniel called out to make sure he could hear himself. In his nightmares, his voice was often silenced. But he could hear. He was okay—awake and alive—for now.

Out of the darkness stepped a large figure, his dress shoes tapping on the concrete as he came into Daniel's blurry field of vision. It was one of Reynolds's henchmen—the one who had smacked him upside the head with a rifle.

"Hey, fuck you, buddy," Daniel said. "I was cooperating."

"You also killed three of our men," the big guy said in a deep voice as he stepped closer. "Now, shut the hell up."

Smack.

A meaty mitt struck Daniel across the face, and pain gathered in the lump on his cheek. He checked out the thug and recognized him as Martin Fleck.

"That's right," he said. "You're Big Marty—Reynolds's personal muscle. Tell me, Martin, what's it like being his bitch?"

Big Marty punched Daniel right in his broken nose. It stung behind his eyes as fresh blood poured out his nostrils.

"Fuck," Daniel stammered. "You pack a punch. Now, how about you untie me so we can settle this man to man. I'm a bit... hampered in this fight."

"Fat chance. Boss wants me to keep you here until he shows up. He told me not to mess ya up any further, but I couldn't resist."

Daniel paused. His brief delirium kept his previous streak of anger at bay, but his mind returned to Sarah. He examined the metal chair he was sitting in and shook it a bit. It creaked. There was an excess of rust along the hinges.

"Hey, Martin?"

"Shut up."

"No, listen, Martin. I have important information for your boss, but I'd rather tell you first."

Big Marty turned around and glared at Daniel.

"The fuck you got to say that I don't already know?"

"Top secret shit. Come closer, I've gotta whisper it to ya in case someone's listening."

He leaned over Daniel and lowered his head within range. Daniel applied a vicious headbutt and Big Marty stumbled back, clutching his nose.

"Ahh, fuck! You motherfucker."

Like a bull elephant, Big Marty charged at Daniel with heavy steps. His hands were stained in his own blood. He picked Daniel up by the scruff of his shirt and threw him across the room. The chair shattered on impact with the floor, and Daniel wrestled himself out of the ropes. Big Marty's eyes widened as he reached for his sidearm. His fat, blood-soaked fingers slid along the holster, and he missed a solid grip twice before grabbing the weapon. In that time, Daniel picked up one of the chair's legs and stumbled toward Big Marty.

Daniel plunged the sharp end of the broken chair leg right into the side of Big Marty's neck. A dark red shower covered Daniel's hand and splattered on his face as he twisted and opened up the bruiser's throat. Big Marty grasped at Daniel and gurgled as he hit the floor. Daniel backed away and watched him struggle. After a short time, the big man went limp.

Daniel broke for the exit. He stopped himself and ran back to Big Marty's corpse, grabbing his gun and a wallet out of his pants pocket. There was almost $400 in there. Daniel took a side door into an alley and stepped in a puddle, inadvertently washing the blood off his shoe. Rain pummeled him from above and carried away much of the rest into the storm drains.

He reached for his phone, but his pocket was empty. Big Marty probably took it while he was out, but no time to look for it now. Daniel ran down the alley and toward a chain link fence, which he struggled to climb before throwing himself over. He landed hard on the pavement and felt a striking pain in his ribs. Was he hurting there before? It didn't matter. *Have to keep running.*

Two streets over, Daniel realized he was in Old Vegas. The lights of Binion's and the Golden Nugget shimmered. Tourists ran by him, shielding themselves from the rain with their jackets and the occasional umbrella. They hardly noticed his disheveled state. Daniel waved down a cab and lowered his aching body into the backseat.

"Where to?" the driver asked without looking back. If he did, Daniel thought, he might have been suspicious.

"Henderson, please. I'll let you know where to turn once we get close."

Taking in a deep breath, Daniel rested his head against the window and watched as raindrops crawled down the glass. The constant stream was slowing down, and dark clouds were heading north of the city. His eyes closed for a brief moment.

After a silent ride to the safehouse, Daniel tipped the driver a hefty sum from Big Marty's wallet. The cab sped off, and Daniel stared at the house from the middle of the street. He saw a shingle loose on the top of the roof and panicked. *Does somebody have the key?*

Daniel rushed to the front door and pulled out Big Marty's gun. He turned the knob and it opened without a key. Someone had been there since he, Andre, and Sarah had left. Panic set in. The veins in Daniel's hands pulsated. He walked down the dark hallway to the living room with the gun raised and whipped around the corner. Nobody in the living room, no sign of anyone in the kitchen, either.

The sliding glass door to the backyard rattled as Daniel opened it. He flipped on the outside lights and saw something scurry across the grass. He fired a shot into the ground and saw that he'd just missed a raccoon.

Daniel slammed the glass door shut and headed upstairs. Nobody in the bathroom, nobody in his bedroom or the closet inside, nobody in the laundry room. Approaching the guest room where Sarah had stayed, Daniel felt a knot in his stomach. He was expecting to see her behind the door with empty eye sockets and a bloody throat—like his nightmare. He kicked the door open. Empty. The bedsheets were still messed up from when Sarah had slept the night before. A lump formed in Daniel's throat, and he lowered the weapon, setting it on the nightstand.

Staring at the bed, Daniel went numb. He pressed his face into the pillow and convulsed in grief, her scent still lingering on the sheets. He stood and made his way over to the mirror, lifting up his shirt to get a better look at his bruised body. His left side was black and blue, and it stung to the touch. Just a few hours ago, he was standing in the same spot, helping Sarah get dressed for the night—her final night. *It's my fault.*

Daniel glanced over his left shoulder and saw the door handle begin to shake like someone was trying to open it. He ran to the nightstand and picked up the gun, pointing it at the rattling entryway. The door stopped moving. Daniel exhaled but quickly tensed up.

With a blast, the door flew open to reveal the dark hallway outside his room. Daniel saw a woman in a red dress—*Sarah?*—walking away from him. Shadows trailed and surrounded her, and her high heels left burn marks in the carpet leading to his bedroom down the hall. She turned right without looking back and opened the door. The light flipped on and she closed herself inside.

Should he follow her? Was he passed out on the couch downstairs, dreaming this whole sequence up?

"Am I awake?" he asked out loud. He slapped himself. He was.

Daniel took measured steps down the hallway, arriving at the door with sweat beading on his forehead. It smelled rancid, like rotten food in a garbage disposal; like the elevator earlier. He heard a giggle from behind the door—childlike, nothing like Sarah's laugh—then a deep belly laugh. After a gulp and a breath through his nose, he reached for the doorknob. It burned a black mark on his hand, and he yelped. Anger bubbled inside him. He pulled the gun from his belt and shot the knob off before kicking the door in. The lights were off, save for a spotlight over the bed. Lying sideways with his head propped up on his hand was Big Marty, wearing Sarah's red dress. It wrapped around his protruding gut and showed off the full length of his hairy, tree-trunk legs. He was wearing red lipstick over a toothy smile and missing his eyeballs. Blood trickled from the orbital holes in his skull. He grinned.

Daniel fired three times into the bed, and the light went out. Big Marty was gone. Feathers shot up in the air where Daniel's bullets had struck the mattress. A loud, crashing noise came from downstairs, and Daniel sprinted to investigate. He arrived at the kitchen to find a knife spinning on the counter. It slowed down, and the sharp end pointed at him like a game of Spin the Bottle. Daniel noticed Sarah sitting on a barstool across from him.

She had her eyes and her throat wasn't slit, but her skin was pale. Her black lipstick matched a skin-tight black dress and black fingernails. Sarah was tapping them on the counter with a cigarette in the other hand. She took a long drag and blew smoke up into the overhead light. Her eyes met his; her irises were solid black.

"So, what's a guy like you doing in a place like this?" she asked.

Daniel didn't know how to respond. He was silent, fear stricken. His gun was at his side.

"It's okay, baby. Take your time: I've got an eternity."

"Who… who are you?"

"Sarah Wallace. Hired gun and woman of the great Northwest. And you are?"

"Daniel," he said, shaking. "You know me. We worked together."

She smiled. It was unnatural, forced by constricted face muscles.

"Oh, I know you, alright," she said. "You're a hopeless romantic. Searching for yourself in other people. But you never find what you're looking for, do you? Always something that doesn't work out, huh?"

Sarah made a throat-slitting gesture with her thumb and laughed. Daniel raised his gun at her.

"I don't know if I'm fucking hallucinating or what, but whatever you are, you need to leave."

"Don't worry, Danny boy. I'm on my way out. I just wanted to pay you a visit. I can come back if you want, looking like this, if that'll please you. Or should I change my outfit? We can make love *all night long*."

Sarah stood up and an opening appeared on her throat. Black blood poured from the wound, and her eyes rolled back in her head, revealing the whites lined with black veins. Daniel fired two more rounds and they hit the refrigerator. Whatever was haunting him disappeared.

All the lights in the house turned back on. Daniel slumped down on the floor and leaned against a cabinet. He tossed the gun aside and buried his face in his hands. Running his fingers through his hair, he cried and sank even lower to lay his head on the tile floor.

The house phone began to ring. Daniel didn't bother getting

up to answer it—just another trick being played on his mind, he thought. It went to voicemail and the voice of his ex-girlfriend came across the speaker.

"Daniel, it's Gabby. Can we talk?" She paused. The sound of cars speeding by echoed in the background. "I tried your cell, but it said it was no longer in service. Are you okay? I was thinking of taking a cab up to the old house in Henderson, but I need to know if you're there."

Her voice began to shake.

"Daniel, please, pick up the—"

Daniel grabbed the phone and pressed it to his cheek.

"Hello, Gabby?"

A sigh of relief from the other end of the line. "Thank God, Daniel. I was so worried. Are you okay?"

Daniel lied, "I'm fine. Just got a new phone, that's all. Where are you?"

"I'm on the Strip. Just got done with my shift at a restaurant in the Cosmo. Started working there this week."

A long pause. Daniel didn't expect he'd have to think of something to say. But he knew he needed her.

"Come over," he said. "Let's talk."

9

A S A LATE NIGHT BECAME an early morning, the desert air took on its signature crispness that chilled Andre's fingers and nose. He had his window cracked for the first part of the drive, but the cold got to be too much, and he closed it. The radio was locked on the R&B station, and as he got further out of town, the soulful melodies of Luther Vandross crackled and were replaced by static. Andre shut off the radio and drove in silence for the final hour.

The sun was rising when he arrived on the reservation. Andre parked his car outside a cabin on the sprawling ranch. He let out a sigh of relief that he'd made it there without incident. His shoulder stung with pain as he reached for the car door and pushed it open. He checked his phone—5:48 a.m.—and figured, *If she isn't awake by now, she's gonna be any minute*. He took wooden stairs up to the well-varnished door and knocked three times. A baby began to cry inside. *Shit*.

After a couple minutes, the door creaked open and Jennifer's head peeked through the crack. Her hair was up, and she was in her pajamas.

"What the fuck are you doing here?" she asked.

"Jenny, I need your help." Andre pointed to the wound on

his shoulder. Much of the blood had dried, and torn pieces of his shirt fluttered in the wind around the visible gash.

"It's not even six in the morning, and you woke up my kid. Why didn't you just wait for me at my office?"

"You ain't open for another couple hours. This needs your attention ASAP."

Jennifer examined the gash on Andre's shoulder before letting him in. Andre followed her to the dining room table. Pictures of Jennifer and her wife—along with their adorable baby girl, who Andre hadn't met yet—lined the walls around them. The baby's crying had ceased upstairs.

"So, what the hell did you get into this time?" Jennifer asked. Andre chose to be honest.

"Robbery went south, some big wig in town sent his boys after us. They kidnapped Daniel and gave me this shit in the firefight. Thankfully, I hid in the tub while they was roughin' Dan up."

Jennifer tore Andre's sleeve open wider and pressed a wet washcloth around the edges of the wound. She poured cold water into the entry point to clean it out. Andre winced. While she fiddled with the needle and stitches, she glanced up at Andre.

"So, who is this guy you tried to rob?"

Andre paused, but he trusted Jennifer enough to let her in on this. Besides, the job was toast anyway.

"Richard Reynolds."

Jennifer perked up.

"The guy who owns all those hotels? Isn't he mixed up in a bunch of criminal shit himself?"

Andre nodded. The worry on Jennifer's face was something he hadn't seen from his longtime associate since they'd gotten to know each other. It made sense, but it gave Andre pause. Did he seem shortsighted to her? Was he wrong to try and quell Daniel's anxieties about the job in the first place? It was Dan's idea, though, so why blame himself?

Andre's face clenched as Jennifer finished cleaning his shoulder and proceeded with weaving in the stitches. For the better part of the last few years, this had been their routine when a job went south, or Andre had caught a stray. He'd drive up to the reservation and—for a nominal fee—get treatment without judgment or the risk of police involvement. Sometimes, Jennifer would come to him. With all these questions she was asking, Andre felt like he was being judged this time around. And maybe he deserved it. *This was some dumbass shit to get caught up in.* Andre wondered where Daniel might be, and how he'd find him.

"There ya go," Jennifer said, finishing up the stitches. "Just keep that area clean for the next few days and don't strain yourself. I'll find an ointment for you to rub in once the stitches dissolve. That'll help with scarring; I know you like when ladies ask about your scars, but this could be a nasty one."

Andre chuckled. "Thanks, Jenny. How's the fam doin'?"

Jennifer walked into the kitchen and searched through a cabinet. She pulled out the ointment and returned to the table.

"They're good, man. Baby's keeping me up all night. She's kind of like you: always bugging me at the worst times. But I take care of her out of instinct. And to be honest, you're starting to make me question the nature of our arrangement, big guy. How much longer are you gonna keep this shit up?"

Andre sighed. "I don't know. This was supposed to be the last big job before we got up outta here. I had beaches in mind, but that shit is way outta question now."

"Beaches? What, like California?"

"Hell yeah. I love it there. Weather just as nice as here but it ain't too hot, and the women are fine as hell."

Jennifer smiled the way Daniel did when Andre went on about the ladies. That conciliatory "aw shucks" look, like there was nothing to be done about Andre's womanizing. Andre had begun to feel insecure recently; like all anyone saw him as was a horn dog. Daniel tried to help him examine it over the years in the heart-to-heart talks they'd shared, but his routines never really collapsed. And he rarely made an effort to break out of them. Andre yawned.

"You need somewhere to sleep?" Jennifer asked. "Guest room is open down the hall. I just need to throw some sheets on that bed."

"Yeah," Andre said, standing in unison with Jennifer. He gave her a light hug, wincing in pain. "Thanks."

Andre followed Jennifer to the guest room and watched her set everything up. As soon as it was ready and Jennifer left, Andre kicked off his shoes and eased himself onto the mattress. He peeled his socks off, took off his pants, and tossed them aside. He sat up and gently pulled his shirt over his head—favoring the shoulder—leaving it on the floor beside his pants. It was still cold outside, and Jennifer didn't have the heat on, so Andre scooted under the sheets and yanked them up to his chin. He let out a heavy breath along with his tension, falling asleep within minutes.

Andre woke from a deep, dreamless slumber to the sound of his phone vibrating. He thought it might be Daniel and ran over to his pants, snagging the phone out of his pocket.

"Hello? Dan?"

"This is call from enforcement department of IRS," a robotic voice said in broken English. "There are pending actions against you and we will contact local cops. Provide social sec—"

Andre hung up.

"Fuckin' robocalls."

He sat up and swung his legs to the side of the bed, leaning forward and rubbing his face with his hands. Dried drool had crusted on his cheek, and he wiped it off with his wrist. The smell of something cooking wafted from the other side of the house. Andre checked the time on his phone—1:30 p.m. His stomach rumbled.

Andre got up and raided the closet. He found a starchy T-shirt and basketball shorts—leftover clothes that he figured Jennifer hadn't donated yet. She was always giving back to this tiny community. Andre twisted the door to the bedroom open and squinted as he adjusted to daylight. In the kitchen down the hall, he saw the baby bouncing up and down in her highchair, gesticulating with glee. Her other mom was trying to feed her something mashed on a spoon, but the wriggly little monster was refusing to cooperate. This was the first time Andre had seen the kid in person.

Jennifer's wife, Sandy, turned around when she heard Andre's footsteps and smiled. Her soft features appeared strained in the face of motherhood.

"Hey, Dre."

"Hey there, beautiful," Andre said, reaching out to give her a hug and a kiss on the cheek. "Bein' a mama looks good on you."

Andre sat at the table next to the baby, who was now looking at him with curiosity.

"What's her name?" Andre asked, reaching out a finger for the baby to grab. She had a vice grip.

"Rose," Jennifer said from the other side of the room. Her back was to them as she chopped up bacon.

"Hi there, little Rosie-poo," Andre cooed. "You just a wild child, ain't ya? Keepin' moms up all night long?"

Rose giggled on cue and shook her little arms again. Maybe Andre needed a baby of his own to settle his life down, he thought. Judging by the bags under Sandy's eyes, though, the life of a parent was a different kind of chaotic.

Andre pulled out his phone and tried calling Daniel. It said the number was no longer in service. He thought about taking the long drive out to the safehouse that afternoon to search for him. Andre tossed his phone on the table and rubbed his eyes. Jennifer walked over with a bacon and cheese omelet in hand, along with a glass of orange juice. She placed it in front of Andre and patted him on his good shoulder.

"Eat up, man. You had a long night."

Andre didn't stop to thank her. He grabbed the fork and dug in, the eggs damn near burning his tongue. The bacon was the perfect kind of crispy, and the OJ tasted freshly squeezed. It didn't matter what Jennifer threw in front of him, he was going to make quick work of it.

Sandy picked up the baby and prepared to leave Andre and Jennifer so they could discuss business. Whenever Andre would come through with an injury and a story, she would stay out of it. She gave Jennifer a glance of worry as she left the room and headed back upstairs. Jennifer was normally a straight arrow, Andre thought. Only bad thing she ever did was take Andre's money under the table for fixing him up.

"So," Jennifer said, sitting next to Andre with a cup of coffee in hand. "What's next for you, buddy?"

"I gotta find Dan. I'm worried. He gave himself up so I could dip, but who knows what they doin' to him. He could be in pieces in the fuckin' desert by now, buried out there with all ya ancestors."

Jennifer rolled her eyes. "He's fine. The way you talk about Daniel, he always seems to have a plan. Although this time that didn't work out so well."

"Yeah," Andre said, shifting in his seat. "The worst part isn't even that we ain't got our money. We got someone killed, Jenny.

Beautiful girl named Sarah. Sent her in there to try and get info outta this motherfucker, and he had somebody kill her."

Jennifer seemed mortified at first, but she took a deep breath and put her hand on Andre's shoulder again.

"I'm so sorry, Andre. How did it happen?"

"That's the thing; I have no fuckin' idea. We watched the security tape and one minute she's on the floor cleanin' up a broken glass this dude threw, and the next, she's on the floor with her fuckin' throat slit. It was nasty as hell."

"So, did the tape skip or something?"

"Nah, it ain't like that. She looked up, scared out of her mind, and she reached for her gun like somebody was comin' at her. But nothin' was there."

Jennifer paused. Her face glazed over.

"And the weirdest shit, Jenny, is that there wasn't any blood or nothin' at the scene when we got there, and it was like a half an hour later. Dan tried to play hero and we went up to that room. Wasn't no pool of blood or stains or anything. I can't wrap my damn head around it."

"And how did you say she died?"

"Throat slit."

"And you're sure this Reynolds character didn't walk over there, grab some glass, and do it himself?"

"I'm fuckin' positive. We saw the tape."

Jennifer paused before getting up and gazing out the kitchen window. Andre stood and joined her. In the distance, Andre saw a massive rock with a path winding up the side. The smooth portions of the rock glistened in the sun. Outside a home across the road, three small children kicked a soccer ball around in the dust. Trees lined Jennifer's property up to the porch, and a horse stable was visible to the right of the home.

"I think I might have an idea of what happened to Sarah,"

Jennifer said, scratching the back of her neck, "but you're not gonna believe it."

Andre raised an eyebrow.

"Fuck you talkin' 'bout?"

Jennifer pointed out a large bird circling above the house across the street. After a moment of silence as they observed its flight, she turned to Andre.

"We need to go for a ride somewhere," Jennifer said. "My dad's house, even further out in the country than we already are."

10

R EYNOLDS SNICKERED AT BIG MARTY'S corpse.
"Should've known better, leaving this fat fuck here with him."

His gaze turned to Oleg, who was scowling.

"C'mon, Oleg, you're angrier than I am. It's a minor setback. We'll find him."

Oleg glared at Reynolds with fire in his eyes.

"And how many more of us will be killed before that?"

Reynolds smacked Oleg upside the head with his cane and leaned close to him.

"Don't backtalk me, boy. Don't forget who pays for that swanky apartment you share with that slut of a wife. She doesn't even speak English. Been in this country, what is it, eight years now? Doesn't speak the language. Lazy bitch."

Reynolds knew Oleg wouldn't dare pop off again. He watched the brute pick up Big Marty by the feet and drag him outside. Oleg grunted and struggled the whole way. The morning sun shined through the metal door to the alley before it slammed shut. Reynolds observed the broken chair and mangled rope in the center of the dark warehouse. A gravelly voice whispered in his ear.

"He's in Henderson."

"I figured. A creature of habit, that one. But he can't hide for long. What's next?"

"Forget about him… for now. Focus on yourself."

Reynolds was puzzled.

"Cut the cryptic shit. How do I get what I want?"

"What you seek is a means to an end. Killing this man is only a small part of your path."

"I'm sorry, but what the fuck does that mean? Didn't I say quit being so damn cryptic?"

"Remember who you're talking to, coward. I'm the one in the driver's seat."

"Pfft… As if. You got what you wanted, now it's my turn. Let's go to that house and—"

Reynolds's body stiffened. Pain reverberated in his chest. Was he having another heart attack? He dropped the cane and was forced to stand at attention. Black smoke filled his field of vision, and a large red hand appeared on his neck, its fingernails scraping along his spine. From the hand came an arm, and from the arm, a sunken chest, long neck and triangular head. The beast's yellow eyes met his, and he struggled to try and free himself from its grasp.

"Pitiful," it said. "Wriggling like the cretin you are. Do not forget who holds the keys to the doors you seek to enter."

"I'm… sorry," Reynolds gurgled. "Let me… go."

The beast released its grip and flicked its tongue in satisfaction. It took a step back and sharpened its fingernails on the concrete floor, leaving behind a trail of burn marks in long, black streaks. Reynolds doubled over and coughed up blood.

"Lung cancer, terrible disease. With the proper treatment, you'll survive long enough to reach what you desire. It's only a single tumor. For now."

Still on all fours, Reynolds turned to the beast. It was breathing heavily, snarling in his direction.

"You did this to me, didn't you?"

"Perhaps. But what is done can easily be undone."

"Undo it now, you fuck."

"Not yet. You need to take your next steps. It's time for you to turn ambition into action."

Black smoke formed at the beast's feet and began to enter Reynolds's nostrils. It disappeared into his head. Reynolds sat up, rubbing his throat. When it was gone, Oleg came back through the door and ran over to him.

"What's wrong, boss? Are you hurt?"

"No, no, I'm fine. Just took a bit of a spill. I'm old, Oleg. Simple shit ain't getting any easier."

"Here, let me help you up," Oleg said, lifting Reynolds by the armpits. He reached down and handed Reynolds his cane. Reynolds snatched it and brushed off his shoulder.

"Let's go. Leave the blood to dry. Won't be any cops sniffing around this place. Where'd you put the body?"

"Dumpster, a few blocks from here. I'll have someone come split him into pieces so they can't identify him."

"Good. He was dead weight, and we're better off without him. This'll do a number on the local restaurant business, though."

The pair walked in silence to the car, a black Lincoln with extra room in the backseat for Reynolds to kick back and unwind.

"Head over to the courthouse, will ya?" he said.

Oleg took the car on a short jaunt down Casino Center Boulevard, past the Golden Nugget, and into an empty parking space in the lot by the courthouse. The sun reflected off the windows of nearby cars and forced Reynolds to squint.

"Why are we here, boss?"

"Important business, Oleg. Now, you stay here. I'll be right back."

Reynolds pushed himself out of the car and slammed the door shut. Taking his time with each step and not straining himself, he walked toward the courthouse. On his right and down the road was a Catholic church. He thought about what his funeral might be like if the cancer took him. Who would show up?

A glass door led Reynolds to a security checkpoint. He grumbled and placed his cane on the metal detector's conveyor belt, removing his gold chain and various rings before setting them in the designated bin. He went through without issue, grabbed his belongings and stuffed them in his pockets.

Making his way through the bustling hallways of the courthouse, Reynolds rubbed his knuckles expecting his rings to be there. It felt naked to be without them, but he didn't want to waste time jimmying them back on. Following the signs, he arrived at a tan door with a small, glass window that read *CLARK COUNTY ELECTIONS.*

With a rush of conditioned air to his face as he opened the door, Reynolds thought the place smelled like lavender. The girl behind the counter had some of it in a small vase on her desk. Reynolds noticed she had perky breasts behind a tight gray polo and a cute face with a sizeable mole on her right cheek. She was on her phone. He tried not to look at the mole and turned on the charm.

"Hello there," he said through a smile. "I'm looking to file a candidacy, please."

The girl's eyes raised from her phone.

"I'm sorry, what?"

Reynolds sighed. "I want to file for a candidacy. I need the form."

"Yes, so sorry. Let me get that for you right away."

She got up and turned to the file cabinet to search for his

form. It wasn't in the top two drawers she checked (*How does she not know where it is?*) and she bent over to dig through the bottom drawer. Reynolds admired the full curvature of her ass and noticed her panty line. He bit his lip and adjusted his standing position to try and appear taller. The cane was hidden from her vision.

"Here it is!" She pulled a form out of a manila folder and rushed over to the counter, slapping it on the surface and handing him a pen. "Fill that out and you should be good to go! Oh, and I'll need $29 from you as well."

Reynolds whipped out his wallet first, handing the girl two $20 bills.

"Keep the change for yourself, doll," he said with a wink.

"Oh, sir, I can't do that. Against department policy."

"I said keep it." Reynolds leaned forward and raised his eyebrows. "There's a lot more where that came from, too, if you're interested."

Her face, once a bubbly smile, went flat.

"Just fill out the fucking form, dude. Not interested in whatever you're offering." She handed him $11 back, and he took it.

Reynolds put his hands up in surrender and made his way to a seat in the waiting room. He got started on the form.

> **CANDIDATE NAME:** *Richard Reynolds*
> **OFFICE SOUGHT:** *Mayor, Las Vegas*
> **PARTY:** *Independent*

With a few more details and a final signature, Reynolds dropped the form off at the front desk.

"Thanks for your help, sweetheart."

"Yeah, whatever. Don't let the door hit you."

Reynolds scoffed and left the office. He tried walking without the cane for a stretch as he returned to the car, but the pain became too much to bear as he reached the crosswalk. He pressed the cane against the pavement and hobbled to the vehicle where Oleg was waiting, eating a cheeseburger and staring at his phone.

"Get me anything?" Reynolds asked as he got in.

"Yeah. Double cheeseburger and fries. No tomatoes."

"Good lad." Reynolds reached into the bag and pulled out the still warm burger. He unwrapped it and took a huge bite, letting the cheese and beef melt over his tongue.

"This," he said while chewing. "Is a damn good burger."

"Best in town. Russian owned."

"Russians? Really? They your family or some shit?"

"No, just friends."

Reynolds grabbed a handful of fries and shoveled them in between his cracked lips.

"Didn't know you had friends, Oleg. Thought you guys just sat alone in hotel rooms, smoking cigarettes and thinking about your beloved *babushka*."

Oleg didn't respond. Reynolds grabbed his soda and sucked down a gulp before returning to work on the cheeseburger. A few minutes later, Oleg broke the silence.

"So, what were you in there for?"

"Filing my candidacy for mayor of Las Vegas," Reynolds said as he took a final bite, sucking the grease off his fingers. "Election is in a few months. This town needs a change, Oleg, and who better to bring it than me?"

Oleg turned back, surprised.

"Mayor? What about the business?"

"The legitimate business? I'll run based on my successes and rake in even more cash if I win. The *other* business ventures can take a backseat for a while."

"But what about this Daniel guy? Aren't we going to look for him?"

"I know where he is, Oleg. I just don't care right now; we've got bigger fish to fry. I'm gonna need your help communicating a few things to my people at The Luxury and the other properties. You got something to write with?"

Oleg searched his jacket and found nothing. He popped open the glove box and found a notepad but no pen. Reynolds handed him the pen he stole from the elections office.

"Okay, write this down. For The Luxury, put out a press release saying the company is hiring cleaning staff, a concierge, and people to wait tables at the restaurant. Cooks too."

"Why do you need more people on staff? Don't you have enough?"

"That leads me to my second point: instruct the hotel manager to do a background check on everyone we've got working in those positions now. If any of them are immigrants—legal, illegal, doesn't fucking matter—fire them. I want the press release to offer the jobs to *real* Americans."

"Boss, you're axing a big chunk of the folks you've got working there."

"Don't care. Third thing is I need you to tell the same thing to the casinos and other properties. Anything with my name on it, I want those jobs going to Americans. Got it?"

"Got it. Why again are you doing this?"

"It's a great platform, Oleg. These politicians, they aren't prioritizing the needs of *our* people, do you understand? I hear it all the time: people are sick and tired of these immigrant motherfuckers taking their jobs. I'm a businessman first, and if I show people that I practice what I preach in my business, that's good for me, okay?"

"Okay, I just…"

"Just what, Oleg? The fuck did I tell you about backtalk?"

"No, I'm sorry, it's just… This is out of nowhere, boss. One minute, we are going after these guys who want to kill you, and now you're running for mayor?"

"This is what I want, Oleg. I've been thinking about this for a long time. I ain't getting any younger, and now is the time to put this great mind to work."

Reynolds pointed to his head. Oleg nodded without emotion.

"Alright then, where to next?" Oleg said.

"Back to The Luxury. I need you to deliver that information to my people around town. We—I have a speech to write."

11

ANDRE TURNED HIS HEAD TO the side to get a better look at the horse's penis.

"Daaaaamn. My boy *packin'*."

The cool morning air blew into the stable. Dust carried in the wind, and the sounds of life bustling in town echoed in the distance. Andre heard Jennifer digging through a chest of supplies.

"Jesus, this obsession with the phallus," she said. "Have you ever seen a horse before, Andre?"

Andre scoffed. "Man, that's racist. I seen 'em. Just haven't... been on one."

"Well, you're about to." Jennifer tossed Andre a pair of gloves. "Put those on and pick a hat from the rack. This is the only way we're getting to my dad's place."

"The fuck? Why can't we take my whip?"

"No roads out that way. And last I checked, your Mercedes didn't have four-wheel drive."

"Don't you got a Jeep or some shit?"

"I have a few ATVs in the garage, but my dad gets real grumpy about tire tracks ripping up his property. Something about 'Leave no trace' or some shit. He's very old school."

"I'll bet. He wear the big hat with the feathers and shit?"

Jennifer frowned. Andre smiled.

"I'm kidding, come on now. So, you gonna tell me how to get up on this thing?"

Andre observed the black stallion from a safe distance. Its tail whipped flies away from its towering, muscular backside. A tan saddle with white accents sat on its back as the horse whinnied and sneezed.

"Yeah, but you need some boots first, cowboy."

Jennifer grabbed Andre some dark brown boots with black accents, spurs spinning on the heels and shining in the desert sun. Andre kicked off his loafers and slipped the boots on. *Perfect fit.*

"Aight, let's get this shit over with. Get me up on that horse."

Jennifer guided Andre over to the horse's side. Andre gave it a nice pat on the side of its neck before leaning his face close.

"Hey there, horsey. We gonna be best buddies, yeah? You ain't gonna buck me off?"

"You'll be fine," Jennifer said. "Now, get your left foot up in the stirrup and swing your right leg over his back. Make sure you don't kick him in the ass on your way up."

Andre did as he was instructed and settled himself into the saddle. He made extra sure he had his bearings before sitting up with confidence.

"Hell yeah! This shit's easy."

"That was the easiest part by far. Now you gotta get him to move for you. I'll unhitch him, then we can practice walking around the stable."

Jennifer let the horse loose, and it backed out slowly. Andre leaned side to side—his limbs were stiff at first. With Jennifer's guidance, he learned how to control the reins and adjust speed. Before long, his horse was trotting in circles around the barn, huffing with confidence. Andre, too, was swaggering about with joy in his newfound skill.

"I'm like *Django* in this bitch."

Jennifer chuckled but kept a skeptical eye on him. Andre slowed up his horse and put his hat on, facing out the barn door. He turned back to Jennifer and pretended to have some tweed in his mouth.

"Let's mosey on then, pahtna."

Andre watched Jennifer hop on her white mare with ease and the duo rode clop for clop out the door and onto the dusty road. They took a hard left and out toward the mountains.

"So," Andre said, bouncing in his saddle and adjusting to the terrain. "What's your dad like?"

"Like I said: old school. He's very wise, very caring for our people. He doesn't come into town much anymore, but when he does it's to deliver his paintings or an important message. He's actually coming to the tribal council meeting in a few days."

"Oh shit, like in *Survivor*?"

Jennifer sighed. "No, Andre, like the actual tribe's leaders. Jeff Probst isn't gonna be there."

Andre chuckled. "Yeah, I know; I'm just fuckin' with you. You don't think I'm that ignorant, do ya?"

"I don't. You're an open-minded guy, Andre. That's why I'm bringing you out here."

As they wrapped around a hill covered in cacti, a handful of rabbits scurried across the valley. Andre took in a deep breath and wondered what Jennifer meant. He was also starting to sweat. The faint stickiness of humidity lingered from the recent rainstorms, and Andre cooked under the sun despite the cool shade of his cowboy hat. His hands were already starting to get tired, along with his lower back. His injured shoulder was sore too.

"What you mean about your dad?"

"My father has a special gift. He can see things before they happen, while they're happening—things that most people can't comprehend. Been that way since I was little. People used to call him a prophet, but as more people of his generation died off, the more skeptical the rest became. Eventually, he didn't feel accepted by some of our tribal leaders, and he decided to move out here."

"What, like he has visions and shit?"

"Yeah. But it's more than that. He senses energies, and he can see changes in the paranormal world, too."

Andre brought his horse to a stop. Jennifer did, too, a few feet ahead of him.

"Your dad sees fuckin' ghosts?"

"If you wanna call it that, yes. He doesn't see the spirits of people, per se, but more like… their feelings; their motivations. People think they're making their own decisions, but my dad can see the real decisionmakers. The things beyond our field of vision that are pulling the strings in our everyday lives."

Andre threw a skeptical look Jennifer's way. They kept riding and got back beside each other.

"Look," Jennifer said. "I know this sounds like a bunch of mumbo jumbo. And frankly, it probably sounds ridiculous coming from a medical doctor. But it's true, Andre. When you get around my dad, you'll see he's not full of shit. Just keep an open mind."

Andre nodded, and they rode in silence for a while. He thought about what had happened to Sarah, how her throat tore open with nothing else visible on the camera. Was it a ghost? Is this trip just another road to nowhere? And where the hell was Daniel?

The outline of a cabin appeared in the distance, and Jennifer rode ahead, turning back to Andre as she picked up speed.

"We're almost there. I'll ride up and tell him he's going to have another guest—don't wanna startle him."

Andre gave the thumbs up and slowed his horse down. He watched as Jennifer hoofed it up to the house and hitched her horse outside. A snake slithered through the bushes on Andre's right, spooking his horse and causing it to kick its front legs up. Andre went flying and landed on his back in the dirt. He ran and caught up to the horse before it bolted, snatching hold of the reins. They walked the rest of the way while he tried to calm it down.

As Andre approached the cabin, Jennifer emerged and hopped down to help Andre hitch his horse. Andre brushed the dust off his shoulders and pant legs. He gave the horse a kiss on the muzzle and ran his fingers through its mane.

"Good boy. It'll be alright. I might have to keep yo ass. Ride around the Strip, showin' off for all the honeys."

"Come inside," Jennifer said with a chuckle. "My dad is looking forward to meeting you."

Jennifer and Andre came through the wooden front door and jammed it shut behind them. Andre pulled off his boots and set his hat on the rack, wiping his hands off on his chest. A blank easel sat unattended in the living room along with painting supplies. When they entered the dining room, Soaring Eagle sat at the head of the table with his elbows on the surface, chin resting on his fists. He stood and extended a hand to Andre.

"Hello there, Andre. You can call me Soaring Eagle."

"Mr. Eagle. Err… Soaring? Nice to meet ya. Thanks for havin' us."

"The pleasure is mine. Please, have a seat. Did my daughter offer you something to drink?"

Jennifer got up from her seat.

"Shit, my bad."

"Watch your language, Jennifer," Soaring Eagle grumbled.

Andre waited in silence with his new, ancient friend until Jennifer returned with water. In that time, Soaring Eagle filled a wooden pipe with tobacco and began to smoke. He puckered a few times and let the smoke waft around his face. An earthy smell made its way to Andre's nostrils.

"So, my daughter tells me you saw something peculiar. Can you describe this event to me: the death of your friend?"

"Uhh, yeah. So, we was... we were working, right? And this girl, our... coworker, she got killed."

"It was a robbery. You don't have to hide details from me, young man. I can see the broad strokes just by looking at your face."

Andre was thrown off. *Is this dude a mind reader?*

"Okay, so we was plannin' on robbin' this fool, right? And this girl Sarah was in there gettin' us info we needed. Everything was normal 'til she get up to his room, and he throws somethin' across the room—a glass. Shatters everywhere, and this girl goes over to clean it up. She's on her knees over in this dark-ass hallway and..."

Soaring Eagle sat forward, setting his pipe in an ashtray on the table. "And?"

"And... she got her throat slit. And it didn't make any damn sense. Wasn't nobody in the hallway with her. The dude she was with was on the other side of the room."

"Hmm," Soaring Eagle said, rubbing his chin. "And you said this hallway, it was dark?"

"Yeah, but we could see her just fine. If anybody was comin' at her, we woulda seen them, too. You think it was, like, a ghost or some shit?"

Soaring Eagle glared at Andre. He couldn't tell if the old man was offended by the language or the insinuation that he sees ghosts. Soaring Eagle's expression relaxed, and he reached out both of his hands.

"Take my hands, Andre. I need to see clearer."

Andre reluctantly placed his hands in Soaring Eagle's. A calm washed over him and he closed his eyes. After a few seconds, Soaring Eagle jerked away from him and jumped out of his seat. Andre's eyes opened, and he saw Soaring Eagle cowering, gathering himself, trying to make sense of something.

"Bro, what?" Andre asked.

Jennifer ran over to Soaring Eagle and wrapped an arm around him. "Dad, are you okay?"

Soaring Eagle turned to Jennifer with fear in his eyes, then to Andre, then back to Jennifer.

"It is exactly as I feared." Soaring Eagle sat back down in his chair and stared with intent at Andre. "Your friend was killed by a Wendigo."

"What's that?" Andre asked.

"A dangerous spirit, one our people have faced many times over the centuries. It feeds on blood, on human flesh, on suffering. It takes hold in the minds of the powerful and corruptible."

Andre thought about Reynolds tasting the blood near Sarah's body.

"So… what? You think this thing took over Reynolds's mind?"

"I believe this man Reynolds is its target. But I do not believe it is powerful enough yet to root itself in his mind. It influences him, has a stranglehold on his psyche, but it needs to feed to grow in power. Your friend, Sarah, was the first offering. I believe it wants more."

Soaring Eagle left the room with haste. He came back moments later with a book, tossing it on the table in front of Andre.

"Open to about the midpoint. There should be a drawing of the Wendigo within."

Andre flipped the pages and came upon a blank box above scribbled words in a language he didn't understand. He held up the pages to Soaring Eagle, whose face became gaunt.

"Oh, no."

"No what?" Jennifer asked.

"There was a drawing there before," Soaring Eagle said. "Where there was once a depiction of this beast, there is no longer. This is how it fends off those who seek to destroy it: with tricks and obfuscation. We cannot see it here because it knows we are aware of its deeds."

The lights in the dining room flickered off, then back on. A glass window shattered behind Jennifer, and cold air rushed across the table. Andre shot up out of his chair and ran to Jennifer. She didn't have a scratch on her, and Soaring Eagle seemed calmer than he should have been.

"The fuck was that?" Andre asked. "What the hell we gettin' into?"

Soaring Eagle extended a hand to Jennifer and helped her up. She took deep breaths like she'd been in this situation before.

"This demon," Soaring Eagle said, "it grows angry with those who shine a light upon it. It can't hurt us when we are so far from its host, but it can find ways to instill fear. Events like this are becoming more frequent as Jennifer and I learn more."

Andre shook his head. "This shit is fucked up." His stomach growled.

"Would you like something to eat, Andre? You must be hungry after such a long journey."

Andre gathered himself and let out a breath. "Yeah, I could eat."

"Great. Jennifer, I have plenty of leftover soup in the fridge from when you were last here. Will you heat it up for us?"

"Sure, Dad."

Jennifer headed for the fridge, Andre and Soaring Eagle trailing behind and making themselves comfortable at the stools along the counter. Soaring Eagle placed a hand on Andre's shoulder. He winced.

"Sorry. It's sore. Took a bullet last night, if you don't mind my sayin' that."

Soaring Eagle examined Andre closer. "It must be a danger-ous line of work you are in, Andre. Have you thought about something easier—or more fulfilling?"

"All the time," Andre said with a laugh. "Yo, Jenny, you need somebody to look after them horses for ya?"

Jennifer poured even portions of soup into three bowls and turned to Andre.

"Nah, I'm good. You stick to what you do best. Not sure I could see you wrangling horses with your appetite for everything the city gives ya."

Andre smiled and nodded. He turned to Soaring Eagle with seriousness in his voice.

"What are we gonna do about this… Wendigo thing?"

Soaring Eagle paused for thought and gazed out the window into his backyard.

"I'm not sure what is to be done. The Wendigo comes around once in a great while, and very little information exists on how to defeat it. I will be speaking to our tribal council this week about that."

The microwave beeped, and Jennifer placed a bowl of soup in front of Andre along with a spoon. Andre took a quick spoon-ful of vegetables and broth and jammed it in his mouth. He burned his tongue.

12

PRESSING HIS HAND AGAINST THE refrigerator door, Daniel felt the cold air escaping through the bullet holes. When he opened it, he found a milk carton leaking out a gash in its side, milk already pooling on the shelf. He grabbed the carton and carried it over to the sink, tossing it in the basin. Out the window, chairs were still set up where he and Andre had stargazed not too long ago. Daniel wondered where Andre was, and if he'd made it out okay. Why did it take until just now for him to think about someone other than himself or Sarah? This was his best friend, for Christ's sake.

A knock at the door startled him. Hustling over and looking through the peephole, he saw Gabby. It was his first time seeing her since that fateful night at the steakhouse, where weeks of tension had exploded in an otherwise quiet dining room. Onlookers went from sneaking glances to full-on gawking as she'd berated him. He sat there and took it, thinking at the time that their relationship was beyond salvaging. He knew he'd fucked up. The question was how long and how loud she planned to call him out on it. It ended up being ten excruciating minutes and a volume far beyond what was acceptable for a high-class joint like the one they were in.

Daniel opened the front door. Her soft features and big eyes glowed under the moonlight.

"Daniel." She threw herself in his arms and checked out his broken face. "What the hell happened to you?"

Daniel thought about lying to her again, but where did that get him before? And what was the point now?

"I was kidnapped. Beat to shit. But I got away."

"Oh my god," she said, running her fingers along his bruises. "Are you safe now? Are they coming after you?"

"I don't know. But I know we're safe here. Nobody knows about this place, and I wasn't followed. Well, not exactly…"

Gabby pulled her hands back from his face and backed up.

"What do you mean, 'not exactly'?"

"Come sit with me. I'm in pain—my ribs."

She followed him to the couch, where he leaned back in agony. He sat forward and coughed. She rubbed his back.

"Daniel, I need you to be okay. I can't be worrying about you even when I'm not by your side every second. How am I supposed to move on?"

Tears welled up behind his eyes. He felt desperate and alone and wished she would reach out and embrace him. But her face was cold now, unfeeling; her concern had shifted to how this situation affected her in the short term. Anger created tension in his abdomen, and he held himself back from blowing up. She always knew how to push his buttons.

"Gabby, I'm sorry. I know I've fucked up in the past, but can't we… patch things up?"

Gabby crossed her arms and scooted away from him. She turned away as tears started to run down her cheeks. Daniel reached out to wipe one away, but she leaned out of his reach.

"You can't keep doing this, Daniel. You can't keep putting pressure on me to forgive you for cheating, or for your emotional unavailability. This isn't going to work unless you change, and I don't believe that's going to happen. You are impossible to love."

Daniel tried moving closer to her. She stood and walked to the center of the room. His head lowered to the warm spot where she had been sitting, and he tugged at his hair.

"You don't understand," he said, rolling over on his back. "This time is different."

"I'm sorry, but how the fuck is this time different? You got busted up and had another near-death experience, and it's given you this magical clarity that I've seen over and over again. Give it two weeks, Daniel, and we'll be right back where we started. I came here because I was worried about you, not because I wanted to re-evaluate a decision that was right for me."

Daniel sighed. He stood up and walked over to the fridge, pointing to the bullet holes.

"Do you see this?"

Gabby examined the holes with concern, then turned to Daniel.

"What the hell have you been doing?"

"I'm being tortured, Gabby. By my mistakes. By the dead. I don't fucking know what's going on, and you're a lot more spiritual than I am. The afterlife, angels, demons—I've never believed in any of that shit. But I'm starting to question that."

She put her hand on his back. "What do you mean?"

"This girl, someone we hired for a job to get info out of someone, she got killed. And I watched the security video, Gabby. Nobody was there to kill her. It was like her throat got slit out of nowhere."

Gabby backed away from him.

"Have you been going to therapy, Daniel?"

He stared at her, disgusted. "No. Did you even hear what I just fucking said?"

"Yes! But what the hell does that have to do with spirituality?

You're all over the fucking place! And you got someone *killed*? Why didn't you call the police? How am I supposed to help you when I don't even know what you're talking about?"

"Just let me finish. Andre and I were robbing someone—Richard Reynolds, the shady guy who built that new hotel—so no fucking way we'd call the cops after what happened. And so, when I get back here, I start seeing crazy, unexplainable shit. The girl who got killed was right here where I'm standing, but she was *different*. Like it wasn't her. Does that make sense?"

Gabby's brow lowered and she turned her head in confusion.

"Not even a little bit. You're saying you saw a ghost? Like this person was haunting you? Are you sure you weren't hallucinating?"

"I… I don't know. But what I'm saying is, I don't think I should be alone right now. I don't know if it's safe for me here, either."

"But at first you said that nobody followed you."

"Yes! But… some*thing* did. I think. I don't know. Can I please stay with you tonight?"

Gabby must have thought he was acting like a scared child. Daniel knew he sounded like one. But no fucking way he'd sleep in this house tonight. And he needed her in more ways than he was leading on. He missed her scent, her warmth next to him while he slept. She might not be coming around to the romantic end of things right now, but she cared about him enough to rescue him from this, right?

She paused, and Daniel could see the gears turning in her head. Gabby finally stared into his eyes—hers a deep green—and nodded.

Daniel woke up next to Gabby and watched her chest rise and

fall. He thought about kissing her awake but knew it would be overstepping his boundaries, even after the few days they'd been staying together at her place. It was still platonic. Her guard was still up.

Lying in bed with her was a victory in itself. He didn't need to make it physical and didn't have permission yet. He sat up and realized he hadn't dreamed in the six hours he was out. That was a relief, he thought, given the nightmares that had plagued him both in sleep and real life over the past few days.

As Daniel's body count grew, regret dug its way deeper into his psyche. The people he'd killed were sticking with him more and more these days. And so were the dead he'd felt tangentially responsible for.

The clock next to Gabby's bed read 9:08 a.m. When he stood to put on a nearby bathrobe, Daniel examined his body in the full-length mirror. His abs were defined with black and blue all down the left side. Bruises patterned his thighs, too, but the swelling in his face had gone down a bit. He tied the robe to cover most of his scars up as he heard her waking up behind him. Daniel turned and watched her sit up, stretch, and turn to him.

"Good morning," she said. "How'd ya sleep?"

"Good, actually. You?"

"Ehh, could've been better. Every hour or two I woke up to your snoring. Had to push you off your back a couple times. Didn't even wake your ass up."

Daniel smiled. It was the first time he'd done it since he and Gabby reconnected. The last few days involved plenty of solitude and sulking.

"Got anything good for breakfast, or am I supposed to buy into this vegan bullshit?"

She glared at him.

"It's not *bullshit*. I'm doing my part to help the planet, and

I'm probably a lot healthier than you. Then again, I haven't been beaten up lately, so that's not entirely fair."

She was in a better mood, Daniel thought. Chipper, even. He missed how she used to roast him like this, how she made him rethink his approach to so many things in his life. Where Andre enabled some of his vices, she held them in check. He figured Andre was probably worried sick about him. How would he find him, though? And where could he have gone?

"Where did Andre end up after everything that happened?" Gabby asked. *Did she just read my mind?*

"I don't know. I gave myself up so he could get out of the situation we were in. I have a few ideas but have no way of reaching him. We've got a policy of ditching our phones after shit like this."

"I know. That's why I was so worried about you in the first place. I knew if you weren't attached to your phone, it must've been serious."

"Yeah." Daniel paused to examine the graduation photo on Gabby's nightstand— a young Gabby in the middle with both her parents on either side of her. Her mother had died last year, and Daniel remembered the toll it took on her. Grief was probably still on her mind, he thought. *Otherwise, she wouldn't even think about sympathizing with me about Sarah.*

"So, you hungry?" she asked.

"Yeah. I'll eat whatever you're having. Vegan diet starts today."

She snickered and left the room. Daniel took a shower, dried off, and slipped on a pair of his old sweatpants that he'd found in her closet along with one of her heavier sweatshirts. When he arrived in the kitchen, a plate with seasoned potatoes, avocado, cherry tomatoes, and fake scrambled eggs was waiting for him. She had melted some cheese into the eggs. *Must be her exception to the whole vegan thing.*

"Eat up," she said, serving herself and grabbing a stool next to him at the counter. They ate in silence for a while. Daniel felt good not having to stress about something. *She really outdid herself with this breakfast,* he thought. Maybe it was time for him to make a dietary change like this.

"This is really good," he said through a full mouth.

"Thanks," she said, imitating his voice with her own mouth full. They both laughed.

"So," Gabby said. "I've got something for you to do today to take your mind off all this crap."

"Oh, yeah? What?"

"Art gallery. Yours truly has a few pieces on display, actually. Remember that painting I was working on of that woman in a field?"

"Yeah! You finish it?"

"Yep. Turned out great. It's haunting stuff. I've also got a couple other paintings and a sculpture there. The other artists are incredibly talented, too. Locals from all different cultures."

"Great. How we getting there?"

"We can take my car. The gallery is at a little spot in the northern part of town by that cemetery and the high school."

Daniel gulped at the thought of a cemetery.

"Don't worry," she said, rustling his hair. "Nobody's gonna haunt you, scaredy cat."

Daniel nodded. They finished up, and he waited in the living room for her to shower and get ready. He clicked on the TV and watched the local news. The female anchor's face flashed on the screen after a commercial for erectile dysfunction meds. She was Asian with red lipstick and a heavy layer of foundation on her forehead.

"Some news in local politics today. Notorious businessman and owner of the Las Vegas Strip's newest development, The Luxury, is running for mayor. Richard Reynolds filed his candidacy yesterday, sources tell this station, and he is expected to run as an independent. Reynolds, of course, has been in the headlines before for his connections to some of Las Vegas's oldest crime families, and his foray into politics is a surprising one for many in the arena. A spokesperson for Reynolds provided a brief statement that the business tycoon will make a major speech tonight in front of his signature hotel. We will bring that to you live at 6 p.m. only on—"

Daniel shut the TV off and stood up in a hurry. He pressed his hands to the side of his head and couldn't believe what he'd just seen. Was this just another hallucination? How could Reynolds do this after everything that had just happened? Why now?

Gabby's heels came tapping down the hallway, and Daniel straightened himself up, trying to act normal.

"You ready?" Gabby asked as she came into sight. Her green dress sparkled and her black hair fell perfectly on her shoulders. *Yowza.*

"Yep, let me get changed real quick."

Daniel traded in his sweatpants and sweatshirt for a green button-up shirt and tan slacks, rushing out the door while he pulled on his second shoe. He matched Gabby as best he could, even if the shade of green was slightly off. After a short drive, they arrived at the art gallery and parked near the entrance. They walked arm in arm up to the door, and he opened it for her.

"*Pour l'artiste,*" he said, bowing to her. She giggled and walked through.

Daniel followed her through the gallery full of stuffy, judgmental faces. He felt like he didn't belong, but they were probably just gawking at the bruises on his face. Gabby led him to the center of a room with wood-panel floors and soft white walls. On a stone column sat her sculpture, a man's head—screaming—twisted to the side with half of it melting away. It was gruesome, he thought, but the details were incredible.

"Damn," he said. "What the hell happened to this guy?"

"It's a commentary on the suffering of man," she explained, "that existence is pain."

Daniel shot her a knowing glance. He pointed at his own face. "Yeah, I'll say."

She smiled, and they carried on. Through hallways and crowds of varying size, they came upon her paintings. The woman alone in the field (*Creepy*), a ship arriving at an ancient harbor, and a bed with rose petals leading to it. The petals became blood stains as they trailed up the mattress, leading up to a massive bloodstain at the center. Daniel thought about his nightmare involving Sarah but shook the feeling so Gabby wouldn't see the worry on his face.

"These are all so great, Gabs."

"Thanks," she said, giving him *the eyes*. Daniel knew the look. He hadn't seen it since long before the fight. His heart fluttered, and something else twitched. An art gallery would be a brutal place to get a boner.

Gabby observed her pieces with pride and led Daniel around the rest of the gallery. Las Vegas's artistic talent was on full display throughout the various rooms, and Daniel was blown away by the quality and variety he observed. In one of the darker rooms near the back, they came upon some of the Native American artwork. Daniel was checking out some baskets woven by women in a local tribe when Gabby called out to him.

"Daniel, come check this out. It's totally macabre."

He walked over to her and froze when he saw it. A horrifying portrayal of a massive, demon-like creature with long limbs. Its skin was red with black fingernails, black lips, and a flickering tongue. Blood dripped from its nails. Its eyes were fixed on a woman standing next to it, her face frozen in a scream, her throat slit, and her eyes missing. A chill permeated through Daniel's body.

"Isn't this badass?" Gabby said. "I wish I could paint something like this."

Daniel's legs were like jelly. The cold feeling stayed with him as he stared at the woman in the painting, and he imagined her mouth curling up into a smile. He began to fall over as Gabby caught him.

"Whoa, whoa, Daniel. Are you okay?" She brushed the hair out of his face. Her face calmed him, and he stood up, gathering himself.

"Yeah, yeah. I'm fine. This painting, it just… I don't know how to explain it. I feel like I've seen it before."

Gabby seemed confused. They both sat on a nearby bench facing away from the painting.

"Did you see something like that back at the old house?"

Daniel took a deep breath and turned to her. "Yes. Like… exactly the same. A woman missing her eyes, just like that. And the slit throat. That's how the girl—Sarah was her name—that's how she died. But we couldn't see who did it."

Daniel sucked in a breath and walked back over to the painting. Gabby followed him with haste and tried to pull him away from it. He shook her arm away and stared at it once more. His eyes were locked on the hideous creature next to the woman.

"I can come back, if you want."

The words of whatever was pretending to be Sarah echoed in his mind. Daniel searched around the painting for clues, then to the informational plaque below it:

"WENDIGO FEEDS"
BY SOARING EAGLE
SOUTHERN PAIUTE TRIBE
NEVADA

Daniel saw a woman with indigenous features dusting off a

sculpture next to him. She was heavyset with a long braid trailing down her back.

"Excuse me, miss."

She stopped what she was doing and smiled with chubby cheeks and bright eyes. "Hi there."

"Hi. Can you tell me how I might get in touch with this artist? His work is… breathtaking."

The woman examined the painting, shuddered, then turned her attention to the plaque.

"Oh, yeah. That's one of the older members of our tribe. I'm Paiute, too. We're scattered all over, but he lives up on the reservation, way out of town."

Excitement and fear mixed in Daniel's gut. "Do you know how to get there?"

"Not really. He's way out from the main town. But from what I know, he comes into town every few weeks to deliver stuff like this. He's a real mysterious guy. Doesn't talk to a lot of people. His daughter is actually our tribe's doctor."

"Really? What's her name?"

"Everybody just calls her Doctor Jen. Don't know her last name. Don't even know if she has one, to be honest. You could try her office, but she only does house calls on the weekends."

"Shit," Daniel said. It felt like a dead end. The name sounded familiar, though. Did he know a Jen? Gabby walked up to the other woman and gave her a hug. They began to chat about the art exhibit while Daniel pondered what to do next. He interrupted their conversation to ask another question.

"Do you know where else I might find Doctor Jen?"

She paused, then perked up. "Oh! There's a council meeting tonight! They start around 4 p.m. in the big building at the center of town. She is usually there since she's so involved in the community. I bet you could talk to her about her dad after."

Daniel gave the woman a huge hug and grabbed Gabby's hand, leading her out of the gallery. He waved back as they left.

"Thanks!"

"No problem!"

Her smile was warm and friendly, but the horror of the painting caught the corner of Daniel's eye. He picked up the pace.

13

SITTING ALONE IN HIS BEDROOM and digging through old books, Soaring Eagle heard two knocks at the door.

"Dad, can I come in?"

"Yes."

Jennifer came through the door. She walked over to Soaring Eagle's desk and leaned over his shoulder.

"What're you reading?"

"More about the Wendigo. There is a method our ancestors used to weaken it: a ghost dance. But I'm not sure it can be killed. It is as though we are kicking a can down the road, so to speak."

"So… the best we can do is force a future generation to deal with it?"

Soaring Eagle placed a hand on his daughter's face. Her skin was still soft, not yet roughened by the curse of old age.

"I can only hope that isn't the case," he said. "We can try this method and hope it weakens the spirit enough for us to drive it out of Richard Reynolds. It is going to take the support of many in our tribe. That is why tonight is so important."

Jennifer paused. "So, are you ready to go?"

"Yes. Give me a moment to meditate on this and we will head into town."

Jennifer left the room. Soaring Eagle sat with his legs crossed in the center of the floor and took deep, measured breaths. He thought about the best way to word his plea to the tribal council, how he could avoid sounding like a crazy old man. He saw political ambition in Reynolds—long-term ambition, the kind that would cause anguish for the vulnerable. Greed, anger, and pain were all down the road if he and others didn't act soon.

A tightness formed in Soaring Eagle's chest. He opened his eyes and it disappeared, but the intensity of the pain lingered in his mind. He stood and went to his window. Lurking in the distance and leaning against a tree was a towering figure with long arms. The Wendigo, displaying an ominous sense of calm, stared into the distance with its back turned to the cabin. Soaring Eagle watched it tap its long fingers along the tree trunk and leave small burn marks in the bark. It disappeared in a thick cloud of black smoke.

"Wicked beast." Soaring Eagle shut his window and headed for the living room. He buried his worry to appear calm and collected. Andre and Jennifer were waiting for him.

"You ready?" Jennifer asked.

"Yes," Soaring Eagle said, turning to Andre. "Thank you for joining us on this endeavor, Andre. We will need your help going forward."

"It ain't no problem, Mr. Eagle. Lookin' forward to it."

The three of them packed into Jennifer's truck and rode to town. She parked a few blocks from the city building, and they walked past shops, small homes and groups of people who were also on their way to the meeting. Everyone Soaring Eagle passed seemed to stare at him, as if his presence was some kind of omen. Soaring Eagle felt insecure in large crowds. As they entered the building, he saw that almost every seat was filled in the tribal council chambers. Councilors sat behind a gray folding table, each of them Jennifer's age or younger, with the exception of one elderly woman. Anxiety welled up inside Soaring Eagle, but through deep breaths, he quelled it.

"Okay, Dad, you should be up right before the public comment section."

After a short wait and other business attended to, the older female councilor spoke up.

"We now ask that Soaring Eagle, a venerated member of this tribe, come forward and speak."

Soaring Eagle stepped up to the podium and lowered the microphone toward his lips. He didn't bring a speech or any notes. He wanted to speak from the heart.

"Thank you for the time you have provided today, councilors. I come to you with information that is of immediate concern to our people. I fear our lives and those of our immigrant brothers and sisters are in danger at the hands of a crooked businessman in Las Vegas. He has been corrupted, and his influence now takes on political ramifications. Richard Reynolds is a candidate for mayor of our state's largest city, and if he were to gain power, he would destroy our way of life."

A young man on the council sat forward and spoke into his microphone.

"And how does he plan to do this?"

"I am not sure. The future is hazy with this man. A number of pathways exist for him. But his intentions are sinister. If he were to gain control of the city government, he would find ways to abuse his power. I fear he may want to develop on our land as well."

A middle-aged female councilor spoke up.

"He doesn't have the authority, businessman or politician. Our land is protected, Soaring Eagle. We are well beyond the times of our forebears who suffered under the greed and excesses of the White man. White men are more often our partners now. They respect what we have out here."

Soaring Eagle cleared his throat.

"With respect, councilor, you don't know this man. While I haven't met him, I can feel the energy that surrounds him. It is a malevolent cloud of smoke that fills his mind. I have meditated on this for some time, and I am confident that he is being controlled by... something; a spirit we haven't seen as a tribe, even in my lifetime. A Wendigo."

A scoff came from where the councilors were seated. The young man sat forward again.

"What exactly are you here to tell us, Soaring Eagle? Should we be afraid of the big, scary White man, or are we being haunted by evil spirits?"

Some in the crowd laughed. Soaring Eagle turned back to Jennifer, whose face had reddened. Andre sat next to her and grimaced.

"I know you may be skeptical of an old man telling stories of the supernatural." Soaring Eagle adjusted his position behind the podium. "But we are in grave danger. I fear—no, I *know*—that a Wendigo has taken hold of Richard Reynolds. The pain he will inflict on us pales in comparison to the pain he will bring to other vulnerable communities. We have an obligation to stop what he is doing for their sake and for ours. Is it not our nature to help those living in squalor?"

Silence fell in the room for a moment. The young man spoke up again.

"We have to worry about our people first. And to be honest, Soaring Eagle, I'm not worried about this man causing problems for our people. Say what you will about our history, how trusting the White man has never been in our best interest, but times have changed. We are far from an oppressed people, at least in this tribe. We may have a lot of problems that need addressing, I'll give you that. Those problems require the attention of the corrupt fools in our state and local governments, but they aren't being caused by magic or ghosts."

Scattered laughter again trickled among some in the crowd. The elderly female councilor leaned toward her microphone.

"Is there anything else you have to say, Soaring Eagle?"

For the first time in many years, Soaring Eagle could feel anger bubbling in his stomach. The skepticism and dismissive nature of so many on the council and in the crowd was infuriating. He gripped the sides of the podium and tried to calm himself. Instead of speaking to the council, he turned around and raised his voice. The wide eyes of his fellow tribespeople watched him.

"Whether you believe me or not, we have a duty as a people," he said. "The politics of big cities and states matters to us. It will impact our lives and our children's lives. You don't have to believe in the Wendigo to see evil afoot. Turn on the news when you get home tonight and ask yourselves: do you feel safe with this horrible man in leadership? If you do, you are a fool. If you don't, join us in our effort to stop him from what he seeks."

Soaring Eagle stomped through a silent room to his seat. He threw himself into the chair and strained a muscle in his hip. He winced as Jennifer whispered in his ear.

"You did great, Dad."

Soaring Eagle nodded. Andre patted him on the leg and gave a thumbs up. The council meeting ended, and the three of them meandered into the hallway. As they headed for the exit, a young Paiute woman with a thin face, big eyes, and a slightly buck-toothed smile approached Soaring Eagle and extended her hand. He shook it.

"Sir, what you said was incredibly powerful. And I just want to be the first to say I believe you."

"You… you do?"

"I do. You are an inspirational figure, Soaring Eagle. My grandparents told me about you—what you've gone through, who you were to them and so many in that generation. You've been fighting for what's right since you were young, and I wanted to thank you."

Soaring Eagle smiled, at last.

"Thank you, my dear. And what is your name?"

"Christina. I work with some other members of the tribe on various forms of political activism. We would like to help you however we can."

The words shocked Soaring Eagle to his core. He'd been taking so much flak from skeptical young people that he briefly forgot what it felt like to have hope in future generations. Turning first to Jennifer who gave an approving nod, Soaring Eagle smiled at Christina.

"Thank you," he said. "Please give your contact information to my daughter. We will meet with you——"

"Dan! Holy shit, Dan!"

Soaring Eagle watched Andre knock people out of the way as he ran to the door. While he was giving a massive hug to a White man with bruises on his face, Andre's shoulders began to bounce up and down, the young man's hard exterior melting away as he hugged his friend.

"Gabby, holy shit! I can't believe y'all are here. Dan, I was so worried about you, bro. Where the fuck were you?"

Onlookers stared at the group reuniting. Soaring Eagle motioned to Jennifer that they needed to head over and introduce themselves. She got a business card from Christina, said goodbye, and joined her father.

Andre, smitten with his friend's presence, calmed down for a moment to provide introductions.

"Dan, this is Jennifer and her dad, Soaring Eagle. Jennifer, you've met Daniel. And this is Gabby, his... our... other friend."

Jennifer shook Daniel's hand first, and he nodded with a curt smile. Soaring Eagle reached out and grabbed Daniel's hand soon after. Electricity coursed through Soaring Eagle's body. Behind Daniel's blue eyes was evident pain, loneliness, and a sense of duty. Soaring Eagle envisioned the ending to this debacle with Reynolds, and it frightened him. He backed away.

Daniel put his hands up. "What did I do?"

"Dad, are you okay?" Jennifer asked, grabbing hold of him.

Soaring Eagle came back to reality and brushed his daughter off.

"Yes. I'm fine. Let me introduce myself to the young lady. How rude of me."

Gabby extended a hand and Soaring Eagle shook it. He saw his painting of the Wendigo on the wall of an art display.

"You strike me as an artist."

Gabby blushed and smiled Daniel's way. Soaring Eagle saw confusion on Daniel's face out of the corner of his eye.

"I am, actually," Gabby said. "How'd ya know?"

"Soaring Eagle has visions and shit," Andre interrupted. "Dude can see the future."

Jennifer threw an elbow Andre's way. Gabby nodded and smiled. Daniel turned his head in curiosity.

"Ever since I was young," Soaring Eagle said. "I have had this kind of... intuition. You have an artist's spirit, Gabby, and I can tell because I am one myself. I also know you two are here because you saw my painting."

"Whoa, whoa," Daniel said. "How the hell do you know that?"

Soaring Eagle smiled and reached to place a hand on Daniel's shoulder but stopped himself before making contact.

"We have a lot to speak about, Daniel. Please, join me and my daughter back at my home. There is something on television we need to watch together, and only then can we discuss what is next."

Daniel nodded, and the group left the city building. They

walked together toward Jennifer's truck until Daniel and Gabby split off to where they were parked. Andre joined them.

"Yo, Jenny, I'm gonna ride with Dan and Gabby over there. I just missed this handsome motherfucker too much."

"That's fine. Just follow us."

"Dope."

Jennifer and Soaring Eagle got in the truck and sat for a moment, Soaring Eagle absorbing the gravity of his last few conversations. What he saw when he touched Daniel's hand had struck him. He couldn't shake the thought.

14

DROPS OF BLOOD TRAILED FROM the bathroom floor to the bed. A mangled corpse was twisted in horror with its guts spilled on the mattress. The woman's hair covered half her face, and her split ends were red and wet at the tips like a paintbrush. Reynolds turned away, licked his lips, and wiped the mess from his cheeks with the back of his hand.

"You know, you could at least let me cook 'em first."

"Has to be fresh."

"Yeah, I get that, but this is so… uncivilized. The broad gave great head, and this is how I repay her?"

"She is meaningless to you."

"Ehh. You're right. But how many more of these we gotta do?"

"Not many. The path ahead will be paved with blood and suffering; enough to feed me for more than one of your lifetimes."

"Whatever you say, man. I don't have much life left."

Reynolds whipped out his cell phone and called Oleg. It rang five times before he picked up.

"Hello?" Oleg said.

"Hey, why you taking so long to answer your damn phone?"

"Sorry, boss. It was… on the other side of the room."

"Whatever. Remember that thing I told you about? It needs cleaning up."

"Understood. I will send the crew up your way. Should they expect you to stick around?"

"Nope. I'm heading into the office. Too much play today, not enough work."

Reynolds put away his phone, grabbed his cane, and left the room without looking back. The image of the woman's body stuck in his mind. He'd seen and done some gruesome shit in his lifetime, but the lengths he was willing to go were getting frighteningly long. On the way to the elevator, he passed the cleaning crew and nodded. He rested his eyes on the ride down.

"It's time to write the speech."

"I fucking know. Where do you think I'm going?" Reynolds responded to the increasingly present whisper in his ear.

Ding. Reynolds exited the elevator and strolled through his casino. A fat, bald man in a tank top sat at one of the slot machines, yellow stains forming under his armpits. Reynolds broke his stride to stop and stare at the miserable bastard. He gestured to a nearby employee to kick him out.

"Excuse me, sir," the young Hispanic employee said. "We have a strict dress code. I'm afraid I'm gonna have to ask you to leave."

"What?" he replied. "Are you shitting me? This is a violation of my civil rights!"

"Sir, if you don't leave, we're going to have to call—"

"Excuse me, friend," Reynolds said, stepping in front of his employee and pushing him out of the way. "I don't think you understand. This is a strict policy that everyone in my casino must adhere to."

Reynolds pulled a small knife from the inside of his jacket pocket and held it to the patron's neck. He froze and stared down at the blade, the overhead lights shining off its surface.

"Please, buddy, be reasonable here. I'll leave right now. Just let me cash out."

"Oh, I don't think so big fella," Reynolds hissed. "You forfeited your winnings when you walked in wearing that miserable fucking tank top. Your fat tits are poking through that thing, and you smell like shit. Stand up and walk out before I make it harder for you to stuff your fucking face."

The man obliged and walked with haste away from the machine and out the front door, peeking back in fear every few feet. Reynolds pocketed the knife and pressed *Cash Out* on the machine. A ticket with $126.49 came out, and he handed it to his employee.

"Here ya go, kid. Think of this as your severance package."

The employee examined the ticket, then gazed at Reynolds with confusion on his face.

"What do you mean, sir? Am I... fired?"

"Not yet, beaner. But I'd be looking around for *nuevo trabajo* if I were you. *Comprende?*"

Anger welled up behind the young man's eyes, and it made Reynolds snicker. *Not going to leech off me much longer, are ya?*

Reynolds patted him on the shoulder and headed for his office. Down a dim hallway and up a short flight of stairs, he arrived at a red door and twisted a key in the knob. Someone had already turned on the lights in his office and left a cigar and a glass of brown liquor on his desk.

"How sweet. And they say all these nasty things about me on TV. If I were so bad, why would someone do this for me?"

A note sat under the glass. Condensation formed a wet semicircle in the bottom corner of the paper, but the message remained intact:

Good luck on this new adventure. You'll always have our support.

No signature, but he recognized the handwriting. This came

from Chuck Hardy in New York. In addition to being Reynolds's strongest connection to organized crime, he also had a fine taste in adult beverages. This was sure to be expensive, Reynolds thought, and smooth as the thighs of a 17-year-old girl. But only a glass? Where was the bottle?

Reynolds took a sip and it confirmed his assumptions. Smooth going down, no burn to speak of. This was cognac. He ran the cigar under his nose and took a deep whiff. Cuban.

"Chuck, you son of a bitch. You know how to take care of this old horse."

"Will he be funding our campaign?" the voice interjected.

"Yes. Fuck off, man. I'm trying to enjoy myself."

Holding a lighter at the tip of the stogey, Reynolds puckered his lips a few times and got it burning. He kicked his feet up on his desk, drink in one hand and cigar in his teeth. A few puffs, then another sip. A cough interrupted his moment of brief pleasure. It stung in the back of his throat. Had he accidentally inhaled? He coughed again, sitting forward and dropping the drink and cigar on his desk. More coughing, then blood in his closed fist. Black smoke seeped out the sides of his mouth before coming out in a steady stream. The beast formed in the center of the room and stared at him.

"Never one for a subtle entrance, are ya?" Reynolds sneered.

"Quiet," it replied. "We are here for one purpose: to prepare your speech. I need to make sure it's right."

"It's my fucking speech. What makes you think you have the—"

Reynolds's chest tightened up again. He coughed and gagged. A black, mucus-like substance came out in his hand. He tossed it against the wall with fear, where it burned a hole in the wallpaper.

"Turn on your computer and start typing," the beast ordered.

Snapping himself to attention, Reynolds obliged. He opened his word processor and cracked his knuckles.

"Where should we start?"

The beast walked behind Reynolds and placed a hand on his shoulder. It didn't say a word to him, but Reynolds began typing. The words flowed from his fingers. Did he control them? Sentences formed in seconds. The message was exactly what he wanted. It hit all the major points: firing immigrants, hiring Americans, creating jobs; humor weaved in between the serious points; charisma, machismo. The people would love him.

"This is fucking great," Reynolds said, lifting his fingers from the keyboard. It was almost done already. "But we need a slogan. Something to drive this thing home."

The beast whispered in Reynolds's ear, "I'll leave that up to you."

Reynolds pondered it for a second, then it hit him:

BRING. BACK. VEGAS.

He stared at the words in the document. Finally, Reynolds could crawl out from the underworld and receive the adoration he craved. Just writing the speech had given him a sense of untamed power. He thought about what it would be like to sit behind the mayor's desk. It made him smile.

"It's perfect."

He turned to thank the beast for its contribution, but it was gone.

"You back in my head?"

No answer. Loneliness draped itself over Reynolds for a moment, but he shrugged his shoulders and hit *Print*.

Reynolds adjusted his tie in the mirror. It was a perfect match to his red jacket, offset by a black dress shirt, black pants, and black dress shoes that shined in the light. He gripped his jacket with his thumbs up and shook it once for posterity.

"Ready, boss?" Oleg asked.

"Ready," Reynolds confirmed

"Ready," its voice echoed in his head.

Outside the front entrance of The Luxury, a podium was waiting, surrounded by a swarm of media members. Cameramen frantically set up their equipment, and a few reporters finished up live shots. Reynolds took a deep breath and pushed open the glass door, stepping up to the podium. A red light appeared on all the cameras. Their eyes were fixed on him. It made Reynolds's stomach lurch.

"Good afternoon," he said. "Thank you all for coming. I just want to start by saying it's great to see so many members of the media here today. With what I've been hearing, I'm surprised you guys didn't boycott this."

A few in the crowd of reporters laughed; most remained stone-faced.

"I'm here today to officially announce the worst kept secret in town: I am running for mayor of Las Vegas as an independent. I'm doing it because I'm sick and tired of these political elites telling us what's best for our city, for our businesses."

Reynolds checked the paper.

"I'm a businessman, as many of you know, and a successful one at that. I've seen firsthand what regulation and hand-wringing and political correctness can do to a business, and I'm seeing that bleed into every decision these spineless politicians make. Businesses like mine are the lifeblood of Las Vegas, and I will bring my success fighting big government as a businessman to my job as mayor. I promise you: I will always fight for the workers who deserve it."

Reynolds flipped the page and raised his voice.

"And those workers are being pushed out of their jobs by *immigrants* coming into our town by the busload to do the jobs so many of our unemployed citizens would kill for. The unemployment rate in this city is fifteen percent. That is *unacceptable*. I promise that under my leadership, we will focus on jobs for *Nevadans*, not these people coming in from who knows where. They are stealing what is rightfully ours, and it's time for us to fight back."

A few reporters muttered to each other. They thought he was controversial now? *Just wait.*

"Now, I know what you're thinking. You're saying, 'Mr. Reynolds, don't you employ a whole bunch of immigrants in your hotel? Your casino? I'm pretty sure one of them served me a cocktail!' Well, not anymore. Effective at the end of this week, all immigrants employed at The Luxury and all other properties under my company's umbrella will have to find work elsewhere. They're fired."

Cameras flashed, and Reynolds curled up a smile.

"I am offering an opportunity for Nevadans—*real* Americans—to apply for these jobs and come work for great wages in a great company. I've got the hottest property on the Strip, and everyone says it's one of the best places to work. Join our team."

Reynolds cleared his throat and flipped the page again.

"Now, this isn't just some big advertisement for my business. You bet your ass I'm proud of what I've built, but that's not why I'm running for mayor. I'm running to give a voice to the forgotten men and women in this town who are sick of being told what to say, how to act or whether or not they can work. To hell with the elitists in city and state government who tell us how to live our lives! It's time to stand up and take back everything they took from us."

Shock washed over some of the reporters' faces. Reynolds

snickered and raised his voice even louder, pointing at the camera lenses.

"If you're like me and sick of this shit, join me at a rally tomorrow at 2 p.m. at the fairgrounds. We invite like-minded Nevadans to come celebrate the start of our revolution. They'll remember the size of our crowd, and they'll hear our voices all the way to the goddamn capitol building! Let's bring back Vegas!"

Reynolds waved to the cameras and ignored the shouted questions. Reporters trailed him to the front door of the building, but Oleg held them off. Oleg caught up to Reynolds as he strutted onto the casino floor.

"Great job, boss. What's next?"

"Get some of the event planning folks together and finish up the details for that rally. And I'm still starving for whatever reason. Have the kitchen send a Reuben up to my room, will you? With fries. And a pickle."

15

THE LIVING ROOM WAS SILENT, filled with unease. Daniel sat forward and scratched his head. From his rocking chair, Soaring Eagle shut off the TV and stood up to face everyone. On Daniel's left were Gabby and Andre. On his right, sitting on the floor, was Jennifer.

"The Wendigo is becoming more powerful," Soaring Eagle said. "The fire in Richard Reynolds's eyes, the anger with which he speaks, the decisions he is making, they all point to the Wendigo's control. The suffering he wishes to inflict, even beyond what he said in that speech, is intended to feed it. This monster's appetite is insatiable."

Daniel stood and gestured toward Soaring Eagle.

"Alright, man. I understand where you're coming from with your belief system and ancient traditions and all that, but have you considered that Reynolds might just be a racist asshole with delusions of grandeur? Did you even listen to his speech? He's just another fear-mongering politician."

Soaring Eagle sighed. "Do not forget, Daniel. You came to me. You saw my painting, and from what I gather that is not the only thing you've seen. Your skepticism is clouding your judgment. Do not deny that which you've experienced firsthand."

Daniel sat down in a huff. Andre turned to him.

"Dan, what the hell did you see?"

"I… After I was kidnapped, I broke out. Killed Big Marty. Got back to the safehouse with only the bumps and bruises you see now. But when I got back there I…"

"You what?" Andre asked.

"I saw something. A few things, actually. Big Marty, missing his eyes, wearing a lady's dress. Sarah, but she was different; something off about her… pale skin and black blood. I don't know if I got whacked in the head so hard that I imagined it or what, but Soaring Eagle's painting… it brought me back to that moment. It's like he saw what I saw."

Daniel's eyes darted around the room, trying to make sense of it all. Soaring Eagle squatted down to place a hand on Daniel's knee.

"Daniel, what you saw was no hallucination. This is how the Wendigo clings to its power. It sows doubt in the minds of those who seek to destroy it, finds ways to break their spirit and drive them to madness. It is no coincidence that you lost your friend Sarah to this beast. It has the ability to see—as I sometimes do—into the future. Only its sight is narrowly focused on protecting the life and reputation of the powerful ones it attaches itself to."

Daniel looked up at Soaring Eagle with misty eyes. "I just feel like her death was my fault. I sent her in there. I played right into that thing's game."

Gabby rubbed Daniel's back. Soaring Eagle grabbed him by the shoulders and spoke directly. "You cannot blame yourself for what happened. You couldn't have known of the Wendigo's attachment to Richard Reynolds. Although the signs were there, you were not raised to be mindful of them. The old ways have come and gone, even within my tribe. Just tonight, they laughed at me, thought I was insane. But the people in this room know the danger we face. And we know that something must be done."

Andre perked up. "So, what we gonna do? Cap this dude Reynolds and skip town?"

Soaring Eagle paced the room and rubbed his chin.

"As I've told you before, Andre, there is no simple solution to this problem. There are ways to weaken the Wendigo, but I'm not sure it can be killed. Its power resides in the power of its host. Financial power. Political power. The suffering this powerful person inflicts. It feeds off it all, so we have to take it away."

Jennifer stood and faced her father. "So where do we start, Dad?"

"With the political power. Call Christina, have her put together as many volunteers as possible. We will begin with a simple protest at Reynolds's rally tomorrow. After that, we can weaken him in other ways."

Daniel left the room. *A political protest? This is what it's come to now?* Robbing, killing, those were his preferred methods. Holding up a picket sign just didn't feel like an effective use of his talents. But at this point, he was questioning everything he thought he believed. This Soaring Eagle character knew things he couldn't have possibly known. This experience started as a robbery—a way to get out of town—and now he was stuck in Vegas, forced to play activist for a cause he wasn't sure he even believed in.

He tossed himself on the bed in the guest room of Soaring Eagle's cabin. Daniel closed his eyes and practiced deep breathing exercises he'd learned from his therapist, back when he went to one. Footsteps entered the room, and Daniel felt a hand wrap around his. Gabby was sitting on his bed, hanging onto him while he kept breathing. His eyes opened, and she cuddled up next to him, her head on his chest. Their eyes met. Words weren't necessary.

Daniel lowered his head and pressed his lips against hers, a gentle peck followed by a few more soft ones, then a gripping kiss filled with passion. She moved on top of him, and pain shot through his ribs. She hesitated, but he smiled at her while she unbuttoned his pants. They grabbed at each other's bodies, rolled around, and peeled off articles of clothing. Daniel ignored the pain in his chest and took control, flipping her over and taking off her underwear. He flicked his tongue, and she moaned. He shushed her, gesturing playfully to the door as if someone might come bursting in.

He worked his way up her naked body for another kiss. He pulled off his pants and underwear and thrust himself into her. They moved in unison, grinding against each other with heat and intensity for nearly half an hour. Daniel lost himself in the moment, forgot about the pain and pressure weighing down on him from seemingly every angle in his life. This moment with her was the only thing that mattered to him now. He finished on her back and rolled over onto his. She cleaned up and they cuddled next to each other, naked in each other's arms, catching their breath and smiling at one another.

"I really needed that," Daniel said.

"I know you did. To be honest, I did, too." Gabby grabbed his face and kissed him. "But this can't keep happening, Daniel. We can't keep falling back into each other."

Daniel sighed. "I know. I'm sorry."

"It's okay. It's not your fault. We both have lingering feelings; I'm willing to admit that. But we have to find a way to be friends without… this."

Daniel smiled and ran his hand along the side of her face. "Do we have to?"

She elbowed him in the ribs. He grunted in pain.

"Oh shit! I'm sorry." She laughed. "I forgot you were hurt. You certainly didn't act like it a few minutes ago."

"You're good," Daniel said, rubbing the spot on his side where she'd elbowed him. "Heat of the moment, I guess."

Gabby pulled the sheets over them both. He pressed up against her and ran his hand along her stomach. Her skin was soft and kept him warm through the night.

When Daniel wandered into the kitchen the next morning wearing only a bathrobe over underwear, Jennifer was cooking up some eggs. Andre was already eating. The smell of breakfast food reminded him of his mother, who was the cook of the family and always got up early enough to whip up something for Daniel and his brothers. He missed her meals and her guidance. He hadn't spoken to her in years.

Andre turned around and ran to him.

"Dan, bro, how you feelin'?"

"Good, man. Sorry we didn't get a chance to talk much last night. I was exhausted."

Andre sniffed the air around Daniel. He gave him that "aw shit" look.

"You and Gabby, huh?"

"No, no. It's not a thing again. We just… had to work out some stress last night."

"Shit, man, I feel you. Glad you got it out of ya. Been a rough week, no doubt."

They sat together at the counter. Jennifer served up some eggs. Toast popped out of the toaster, and Jennifer spread peanut butter on it and tossed it on Daniel's plate.

"You got orange juice?" Daniel asked.

"Yeah," she said. "Here ya go."

A cold glass of the pulpy stuff. He chowed down while Andre stared out the window. Daniel turned the same direction and saw Soaring Eagle outside, smoking a pipe and staring at the sky.

"So how the fuck you get away from Reynolds?" Andre asked.

Daniel snickered through a bite of toast. He chewed and swallowed.

"I got Big Marty pissed, right? So he throws my ass across the room and the chair I was tied to broke apart. Grabbed a piece of it and stuck it in his throat. It was messy."

"God damn. That's some *John Wick* shit right there."

There Andre went again, referencing some action movie. Sometimes Daniel wondered if Andre saw their lives as the plot of one of his favorite films, that everyone had a role to play until they rode off into the sunset. That happy ending seemed increasingly unlikely as time progressed.

"So," Andre said. "Soaring Eagle talked to some girl in the tribe about a protest. We gonna do what these people call a ghost dance. Basically, get in a circle and chant and shit. Apparently, they did this way back and it got rid of that Wendigo thing."

Daniel took a sip of orange juice and raised an eyebrow to Andre.

"A fucking dance? That's how we're going to solve this? How we're going to get back at the guy who killed Sarah?"

"To start off, yeah. Mr. Eagle got all these plans for what we gonna do after that. He said, 'There will be many steps, young padawan,' or some shit like that. Dude reminds me of Yoda. Only he don't talk backwards."

Daniel chuckled and finished his last bite of eggs. He handed the plate back to Jennifer.

"Sorry about this guy," Daniel said, gesturing to Andre.

"It's cool," she replied, washing off the dish in the sink. "I'm used to his bullshit by now. He and I go way back, remember?"

"That's right. I always forget. We've met before, right? You're married to that Sandy chick?"

"Yeah, we've met before. And yeah, Sandy just had our

baby girl. Rose. She's the light of my life. Changed my entire perspective."

Daniel thought about what would happen if he got Gabby pregnant, if they raised a kid together. It sounded sweet at first, but then he remembered their arguments, the volatility that frayed everything. He thought about that happening in front of a kid and was reminded of his parents. Look where he ended up. Would he want to repeat the cycle and do that to another kid? Hell no.

"That's great," he told Jennifer. "Glad you've got the domestic paradise going on."

"Oh, it's far from paradise. I haven't slept in weeks. But for far different reasons than you two."

Andre and Daniel both snickered. Daniel heard Gabby walking in and turned his head quickly. She was wearing his button-up shirt as a dress.

"Hey, Gabs," Andre said. "How you doin'?"

"Hey, Andre. Feeling good. You?"

"Not as good as you, but I'm chillin'," he said with a wink.

Gabby faked a glare at Daniel before smiling and pecking him on the cheek. She served herself the last of the eggs while Jennifer headed to the backyard, presumably to talk to her dad. Gabby ate in silence while Daniel and Andre got ready.

Daniel showered and put his pants from the day before back on. He wrapped his belt through the loops and fastened it before he realized his shirt was missing. Gabby still had it on. He returned to the kitchen and found her, reaching his arms around her waist from behind and kissing her neck. She relented a bit and turned to him.

"Quit it. What do you want?"

"Need my shirt back, ma'am."

"What, right here? And go topless in this old dude's house?"

"I'm sure he wouldn't mind. Might be a fun surprise. Might turn him on."

"Shut the fuck up."

Soaring Eagle came through the door. Daniel shot Gabby a glance, and she rolled her eyes.

"Daniel, Gabby, are you ready to leave?"

"Not quite," Daniel said, pointing a thumb at Gabby. "This one needs to give me my shirt back."

"Oh, you won't need it. In fact, all the men in our group will have painted chests for this protest."

Daniel laughed in disbelief before shrugging his shoulders in acceptance.

"Alright, then. The ladies gonna be shirtless, too?"

Gabby glared at him again. He was pushing his luck.

"No," Soaring Eagle said with a laugh. "Sorry to disappoint you, young man."

Daniel nodded, and Gabby left to change. When she returned and Andre was ready, they left Soaring Eagle's home and packed into a car together. They followed Jennifer's car to a home closer to town, where a group of young men and women were waiting outside in traditional Native American garb. *Like we're going to war.*

Daniel got out and approached the woman Soaring Eagle mentioned.

"Hi there, I'm Christina," she said. He shook her hand.

"Daniel. I think you've met Andre."

"Yes. If you two will go over there with Jacob to get ready, I'll take… what's your name?"

"Gabby," she said.

"Gabby. Great. Come with me, and we'll get set up with the other girls. Daniel, Andre, hurry over there and get painted up."

Daniel and Andre, shirtless, walked over to the man she'd called Jacob. He was the silent, stern type, and without warning, he dipped a thumb into a bowl of paint. It had the appearance of red clay, but not as thick or pasty. It went on Daniel's chest smoothly in various, weaving patterns. Andre smacked a different man's hand away when his thumb trailed around the ridge of his muffin top. *Andre's been gaining some weight lately.*

When they were done, Daniel and Andre turned to each other and burst into laughter.

"What the hell did we get into, man?" Daniel asked.

"I don't know, bruh. This shit feels like cultural appropriation, though, you feel me?"

"Yeah, but they seem cool with it. Even if none of them are talking to us."

Jacob stared at them with a stone face and gave them a thumbs up.

"Aight, Dan, let's go," Andre said.

They met Gabby back at the car. She had a crown of feathers and a traditional outfit from head to toe. She wore the shit out of it. Her midriff was on full display, and the skirt hugged her ass. Daniel's chest fluttered.

"You look great, Gabs," Andre said.

"Thanks. Let's get the hell out of here and get this over with. Not how I imagined my weekend, guys. Not gonna lie."

Daniel smiled, but he worried for Gabby's safety. *She can take care of herself,* he thought. *But so could Sarah.*

16

ANDRE STUCK HIS HAND OUT the car window and let the air blow between his fingers. Cacti and brush speckled the desert landscape. He turned to Daniel, who was slapping his hand on the steering wheel along with the beat. This was one of Daniel's favorite rap songs, and he took care to skip over the N-word whenever he sang along. Andre appreciated that about him. It was the little things Daniel did to respect Andre's background and upbringing that brought the two of them closer. Before they met as teens in Sacramento, Andre didn't know anybody in town. Daniel was the first one to invite him to come play basketball with some of the neighborhood kids, and their friendship was built from competitive moments on the blacktop.

"Dan, you remember that dude we used to hoop with when we was kids: Larry Gordon?"

Daniel lowered the volume on the music. "Yeah, that guy was an asshole."

"This dude Reynolds. He reminds me of Larry's dad. You remember him? Real racist, ignorant motherfucker. Got mad when he knew Larry was hoopin' with us. Probably because of me."

"I remember him, and it wasn't just you. We were a bunch of

punks, and that rich jerkoff didn't want his kid hanging around us. In retrospect, he was probably right."

Andre chuckled. "Yeah, we was some fuckups."

After a beat of silence, Daniel turned the volume back up. Andre twisted his head toward the backseat and watched Gabby on her phone, scrolling.

"How's the phone club?" Andre asked.

Gabby glared at him.

"It's fine. Unlike you guys, I don't cycle through burners. This is the new iPhone."

Andre scoffed. "I don't mess with that consumerism, Gabs. I don't buy into that capitalist hype train, blowin' my stacks on the latest thing somebody tells me to get. Free yourself from the shackles 'round your wrist, baby girl. And start by gettin' rid of that thing."

Daniel turned back to Gabby. "He's a socialist now. Just roll with it."

"I can tell. Good for you, Andre. Power to the people." She held up a fist.

"We 'bout to give it back to 'em today," Andre said, nodding his head and gazing out at the road. "Or at least try to."

Daniel pulled into the fairgrounds and weaved into a parking space in the dirt lot. Their sedan sat in the shadow of a white pickup truck with dirt on its underside and two large American flags posted in its bed. Andre observed a "Blue Lives Matter" and a faded "Obummer" sticker on the back window and rolled his eyes.

"These aren't exactly our kind of people, are they, Andre?" Daniel asked.

"Nah. Fuck this, man. I might be the only Black man in this place."

"True. But you'll be surrounded by the only Native American dudes in there, too. Solidarity."

"That ain't the same, bro. These motherfuckers will notice a Black man a hell of a lot quicker than anything else."

Andre, Daniel, and Gabby walked step for step together toward the entrance to the main stage. As they approached the gate, they were joined by their crowd of allies from the Southern Paiute tribe.

"Hey there, friends," Christina said with a wave. "You ready to raise some hell?"

"Oh yeah," Andre said, giving her a side hug. "Let's get it."

Christina led the group through security, and they found a spot along the left-hand side of the crowd near the stage. A podium was set up with American and Nevadan flags hanging behind it. Andre's anxiety spiked from some of the crowd's eyes following him. There were more people in attendance than he'd anticipated. Country music blared over the speakers, and Reynolds's supporters bobbed their heads or chatted with one another. After an extended wait outside in the heat, the music went quiet and a voice came over the loudspeakers.

"Thank you all for coming today. Allow us to welcome you to our campaign kickoff rally. Without further ado, here's the man himself: Richard Reynolds!"

Andre watched the old man come around a corner from behind the stage in an all-black suit and sunglasses. His cane had a diamond handle (*Damn!*) and he waved to the crowd with a liver-spotted hand. The crowd hooted and hollered. Anger built in Andre's stomach. This was the guy with Sarah's blood on his hands, an entitled piece of shit who didn't deserve any of this wealth or notoriety; a murderer and a thug. Andre peered at the security guards standing at the front of the stage. They were all strapped with pistols on their hips.

"Okay," Christina said to the huddled group. "Let's get this started as soon as he finishes his opening lines. That'll throw him off, for sure."

"Hello, real Americans!" Reynolds bellowed. "How the hell are we doing today?"

"GOOD!"

"That's good. I'm a bit hungover, I'll admit it, but let's do this thing."

Guffaws and chortles filled the air. The crowd hung onto his next few words.

"I'm here today to kick off our campaign for mayor of Las Vegas—to give fine people like you the representation you deserve. I don't know about you folks, but I am sick and tired of these political elites telling us how to live or what we can and can't say. Well, here's what I have to say: Fuck 'em."

The crowd roared. Reynolds smiled and turned to one of his henchmen, raising his eyebrows.

"And let me tell ya something else. I look out in this crowd and see the faces of hardworking people who have been left behind. The people in power right now, I hate to say it, they care more about giving away jobs to immigrants than to you fine folks."

"BOOOOO!"

"That's right! I don't like it, either. But we're gonna bring a stop to that when I'm in office. First thing I will do is make sure every American citizen in this town has a job. We bring in too much money from tourism to toss our people aside in favor of these lazy immigrants. That's why at my business, starting very soon, we won't have a single immigrant employed on our staff. Those jobs will go to you guys, like they should!"

More cheers. Christina nodded to Andre and Daniel, who readied themselves by stretching their necks and shaking nerves out of their fingertips.

"So let me tell ya a little bit about myself," Reynolds continued. "I was born in a small town in Illinois in a dirt-poor neighborhood…"

Andre joined hands with Daniel and Gabby at the far edge of a massive circle. Together, the protestors began to chant and dance. Andre went with the flow and figured Gabby and Daniel did too, as none of them had learned the steps to this ancient ritual. The "ghost dance," as Andre learned, was created by the Paiute people to drive out evil spirits by conjuring up the strength of their ancestors. Soaring Eagle stood at the center of the circle, waving to the sky and crying out in his native language. The crowd's eyes turned to them as Christina held a megaphone to her mouth.

"Richard Reynolds!" she yelled through the speaker. "The Native peoples of Nevada reject your hateful message. We stand with our immigrant brothers and sisters in their time of need and call on you to end your despicable rhetoric!"

Boos rained down from the horde of supporters. Food and drink began to fly in their direction as Andre tried to keep up with the steps. He saw Reynolds turn toward them with a disgusted look on his face—pure fury and anger. Reynolds gestured to his men to take care of them before turning back to the crowd.

"Don't worry about these people, everybody. I shouldn't even say *people*. Just listen to 'em; they're fucking savages."

More laughter from the crowd. A few supporters came over to the circle of dancers and pushed one of the Paiute men to the ground.

"Go back to your fucking teepee, redskin piece of shit!" one of them yelled.

The Paiute man didn't respond. Someone spit in his face as he got up, but he wiped it off and returned to dancing. Andre wanted to beat the hell out of the guy who had pushed him, but the coward scurried back into the crowd before Andre could make a move.

"Look, fellas," Reynolds said, directing his speech at the

protestors. "The pow wow isn't until next week. You've got your dates all wrong."

A few muscular men in suits arrived at the crowd of protestors and began to rough up the group. They all put their hands up and didn't fight back, but Andre really wanted to. Andre's gaze turned to Soaring Eagle, who was frozen in the center of their weakening circle. His eyes were filled with fear.

Andre whipped his head around to see what Soaring Eagle might be looking at. Nothing seemed out of the ordinary. When he turned back toward the center, he saw it: a tall, gangly monster with bright red skin and long fingers hanging below its knees. Its fingernails were black and scraped back and forth on the ground, leaving behind burn marks. It was hunched over, standing in front of Soaring Eagle at the center of the circle, breathing heavily. *The Wendigo.*

Andre tried to grab Daniel, but he was busy yelling at one of Reynolds's men for putting his hands on Gabby. He searched around for signs of panic and, inexplicably, nobody else in the crowd seemed to notice the Wendigo. It took heavy steps closer to Soaring Eagle, who stared up in disbelief. It raised a hand in the air, and everything around Andre became silent. He watched as the Wendigo extended its right index finger in Soaring Eagle's direction. It plunged the finger into his chest. Soaring Eagle grabbed at the spot. No blood, no wound, but he was in visible pain. The Wendigo turned back to Andre and smiled. Its teeth were sharp and rotten. Its eyes glowed a bright yellow, even beneath the daytime sun. The eyes were the last thing Andre saw before the Wendigo disappeared in a cloud of black smoke. Soaring Eagle collapsed to the ground.

"Dad! Dad!" Jennifer yelled, rushing to her father's side. She lifted Soaring Eagle's head, and his eyes were wide, lifeless. His body was stiff. Jennifer began to cry into Soaring Eagle's chest. Andre ran over to try and help but was tackled by one of

Reynolds's men. He turned over on his back and received a swift punch to the jaw. Andre returned it with a blow to the throat, and the big man doubled back, clutching at his neck and gasping for air.

Hanging from the man's belt was a holster with a pistol. Andre hoped it was loaded. He pushed himself out of the dirt and ran over to the gasping henchman. Reaching for the weapon, Andre threw an elbow with his right arm and grabbed the gun with his left. He raised it toward the stage, and the crowd gasped and screamed.

Silence again. Andre watched Reynolds's eyes grow wide as some of his men rushed to protect him. But they weren't quick enough. Andre fired three rounds, and two caught Reynolds in the chest. Reynolds fell back into the arms of his security detail. The crowd began to flood the exit. Sound returned to Andre's ears, and he heard massive footsteps coming from behind him. He couldn't turn in time to evade the open-field tackle from one of Reynolds's men. A shoulder struck Andre in the chest, and he went down, dropping the gun.

The brute's weight holding him down, Andre clawed for the gun that was just out of his reach. He was pummeled with punches from the man's hulking fists. Blood poured from his nose and mouth. He raised his arms in surrender and spoke up.

"Wait, wait!" Andre coughed. He turned his eyes toward the exit and watched Daniel help Jennifer drag Soaring Eagle's body out the front gate. Tears were streaming down Gabby's face as she pointed back at Andre, but Daniel said something to her and they moved along.

Andre turned his attention to the enormous Black man on top of him. He snickered at his bald brown head as it shined in the sun, eyes bugged out and neck fat jiggling. Sweat dripped off the man's face onto Andre's. He was shaking, unsure what his next move should be. Andre laughed and leaned his head back in disbelief.

"The… the fuck you laughin' at?" the man spat down at Andre.

"Nothin', homie. I just killed your massa, that's all. You one of his house niggas?"

Andre felt knuckles hit his forehead and lost consciousness.

17

DOCTORS AND NURSES SCRAMBLED AROUND Reynolds. They pushed him down a hallway on a gurney, hands wiping and pressing and tearing open his shirt. His eyes rolled back in his head. Small hands gripped his clothes and dragged him down through the floor. Screams of children filled his ears and grew louder as he got lower. It was hot. His back began to burn as he shot up out of bed.

Reynolds shook his head and saw the room: his childhood bedroom in the suburbs of Chicago. Snow piled up outside the windowsill, and a cold breeze leaked through the cracks in the caulking. He shivered and noticed his legs were shorter. And his hands were tiny. He was a child again.

"What the fuck?" he said in a squeaky voice.

His mother burst in, wearing an apron stained with whatever she was cooking for dinner. Heavyset with strong arms ("mama arms," she used to call them), she was sweating and had her hair up.

"Richie, it's time for supper. Come before your father gets impatient."

"Yes, mama," Reynolds replied involuntarily. He searched around the room again just to make sure he wasn't losing it.

His mom disappeared from the doorway, leaving behind a trail of black footprints into the kitchen. He followed them around the corner and arrived in the dining room, where his father was waiting with a cigarette in his mouth. He wore a gray wifebeater over tan, vascular skin and had slicked-back hair colored a deep black. It was Reynolds's father but older than he remembered from this point in his childhood. Reynolds pulled up a chair next to him.

"Cigarette, Richie?" he croaked.

"No, Daddy. Mommy says those are bad for you."

Reynolds's father leaned closer to him, blowing the smoke in his face. It smelled of burning flesh. Reynolds coughed and cowered at his father's aging face, sinking with time.

"You think I give a *fuck* what that heifer thinks?" he spat at Reynolds before leaning back in his chair. Reynolds's mother came around the corner with two plates of food.

"Supper's up, boys," she said, setting them down. On the plate was stuffed chicken breasts with a side of pasta and broccoli.

"I want you to eat all your broccoli this time, Richie."

"Yes, mama."

Silence, save for the clanging of forks and knives on plates. Reynolds's mother sat quietly with her arms crossed, gazing off into the distance. She didn't have food for herself. Reynolds wondered why. He worried about her.

His father lifted up a piece of pink chicken with his fork, staring at it in the yellow light that hung above their dinner table. He shook in anger before flicking the piece of chicken at Reynolds's mother, who flinched.

"You call this chicken, you fat bitch? One job—one fuckin' job—and you can't even do that right. The hell's the matter with you?"

"I'm sorry, Joseph, I…"

"Save the backtalk if ya know what's good for ya," his father said, tossing the plate across the table to her. "Throw this shit in the fuckin' garbage."

Tears flowed down Reynolds's mother's face as she grabbed both plates from the table and hurried out of the room. Reynolds turned to his father in anger.

"Why the hell do you have to be so mean to her?"

Slap. A sting across Reynolds's face.

"Don't you fuckin' start too, ya little brat. Now wake up, will ya?"

"Wha-what?"

"Wake up, Mr. Reynolds. Wake up. Wake…"

His father's eyes poured out of his skull and onto the dinner table, splattering everywhere. His jaw went slack, and black liquid poured from his gullet. His dyed-black hair went white. A twinge shot up Reynolds's spine, and he closed his eyes tight.

They twitched back open to the white light of a hospital room. A doctor stood next to him, examining his face. Reynolds tried to stay awake but was being dragged down again. His eyes darted across the room, and he noticed the beast sitting cross-legged in the guest chair to his left. It twiddled its thumbs and made eye contact with Reynolds. It winked with a crooked smile. He passed out.

Reynolds was alone again, surrounded by blackness. He was himself this time—his older self—but he didn't need the cane to walk. He meandered around the darkness without pain, but he was struck with anxiety. Nothing in any direction. A slight whisper in his ear.

"Where do you think you are?"

"That's what I'm trying to figure out. Oh, god, what is this?"

"This is your final resting place," the voice said with a snicker.

"Fuck, am I dead? That fucking guy shot me… during my speech. That's how I went?"

"No, no. You are still clinging to your body, at least for now. But one of the bullets pierced your lung. You are breathing through a machine. I'm watching you now."

"You again? How the fuck are you in here, too?"

"I'm always here. But you're going to have to do this next bit yourself."

Through the darkness, Reynolds could see a pinhead of light in the distance. He ran toward it, but the light remained far away until it disappeared. Darkness filled his field of vision again, and he sank to the ground. He sat with his face in his hands. A tap on his shoulder startled him—a child's hand. Reynolds whipped his head around to see who it was, but nobody was there. A giggle echoed from the left, and he saw a little boy skipping away from him. His skin and clothes were gray, like an old movie.

Reynolds followed him, running with a speed he hadn't had since his youth. When he finally caught up to the kid and swung him around, the boy's face was locked in an unnatural smile. His cheeks seemed like they were about to burst, he was smiling so hard.

"Thanks for what you're doin', Mr. Reynolds!" the kid said with cheer. "I sure am excited for my future!"

"You're uh… you're welcome, kiddo."

"You wanna come with me to meet the others? They're real excited about what you've been doin', too!"

The kid grabbed Reynolds's hand and dragged him along. His attempts to resist were met with a stronger pull from the kid, who refused to let go. Before he realized what happened, they were in a log cabin, a fire crackling in the fireplace. A black metal door at the back of the room caught Reynolds's attention.

"Where does that go?" he asked the kid. Reynolds glanced

out the window and saw the vast expanse of wilderness sur-rounding the cabin. It calmed him, if only for a moment.

"Oh, that door? That's where everybody else is. Come on! Let's go meet 'em."

Reynolds followed the kid through the black door into a smoky room. Frank Sinatra's "I've Got You Under My Skin" was playing over a speaker. As the smoke cleared, Reynolds observed four blackjack tables set up, one in each corner of the room. At the center was a bar where a man with a curled-up mus-tache served cocktails to a pair of beautiful women, who glanced in Reynolds's direction. One of them had tremendous cleavage. Reynolds noticed he had a raging hard-on.

"Might wanna put that thing away, mister," the kid said.

Reynolds felt uncomfortable and checked his pants. His erection was gone. They arrived at the blackjack table in the far-right corner and Reynolds lowered himself into a chair. He groaned like he'd been walking forever. His bones started to feel old again. A cane appeared next to him, leaning against the wall. It was his new one with the diamond head, but blood was splattered across the diamond's shiny surface. It dripped onto the floor like it was still fresh.

"You jumping in?" the dealer—a heavyset Hispanic man—asked Reynolds.

"Yeah," Reynolds replied, pulling cash out of his pocket that he didn't know was there. The dealer handed him a fat stack of chips, and the game began. Reynolds kept winning hand after hand until it was just him and a woman wearing a veil. He couldn't get a good look at her face, but her ass barely fit on the stool, and her breasts seemed ready to pop out of her red dress. Reynolds felt another erection—a huge one—hit the underside of the table. It tipped the table up at an angle, and his chips slid across the felt along with a handful of cards.

"Excuse me, boss, but we're trying to finish a game here,"

the dealer snapped. He glared at Reynolds with fire in his eyes. The table fell back to its normal position, and the dealer put everything back in place. Reynolds was afraid to turn to the woman again, until she reached out a hand and touched his arm.

She unfurled the veil, revealing ruby red lips and blue eyeshadow that didn't match what she was wearing. That threw Reynolds off until he saw her neck. Her throat was slit, and blood poured out on the table, darkening the bright green felt and soaking the white cards a deep shade of red.

"Sir, why did you do this?" the dealer asked, grabbing Reynolds's face. Reynolds pushed his hands away.

"The fuck do you mean?" he said. "This wasn't me. I don't know nothing about this."

"But that's the thing, *compadre*. You do. It's your doing. You let it do what it wanted. And now look at her."

Sarah was slumped over the table. Her body began to contract off the edge, and her head turned upwards. The hole in her neck opened wider, and blood sprayed all over Reynolds's shoes. With an unforgettable *snap* followed by a *thud*, her head separated from her body and rolled across the table into the dealer's hands. He lifted her head up by the hair and presented it to Reynolds.

"This is the cost to play, Richard," the dealer said. "You got *this* in your fucking pockets?"

Sarah's face contorted into a smile. "Come on, baby. Let me suck that big dick of yours."

Reynolds tried to get up and back away from the table, but his foot slipped, and the stool fell backwards. He hit the floor and opened his eyes in a comfortable chair behind a large desk.

"Oh god, please, no!"

"Sir! Sir, are you okay?" a young man in a suit said, rushing over to Reynolds's desk.

He examined the room and couldn't believe where he was:

the Oval Office. Just how it was portrayed on TV—a portrait of George Washington on the wall, couches and chairs in the center, and large windows behind him. He sat behind the Resolute desk with little American flags and stacks of papers in front of him alongside ballpoint pens in a mug with the presidential seal.

"Yes, I'm fine," Reynolds replied, gathering himself. "Just dozed off is all."

The young man pressed a finger to his earpiece. "The Gambler is secure. No issue here."

Giving a thumbs up and a forced smile, the Secret Service agent left the room. Reynolds took a heavy breath and leaned back in the chair. He felt safe at last. He rested his eyes for a moment when someone burst into the room.

"Mr. President, urgent news from New York," a woman said, rushing to his side with a laptop in hand. She placed it on the desk in front of him and played a video. It was shaky cell phone footage of Times Square, a massive crowd of people screaming and scattering. The video panned up to the sky from where a large missile came hurtling toward the ground. It struck, and the video cut out.

Reynolds was drenched in sweat. He panicked, searching for something to drink. One of his aides handed him a glass of whiskey on the rocks. He kicked it back and stared blankly at the screen, then to the woman showing him the video.

"What happened?"

"A nuclear attack on New York City. Millions are feared dead, Mr. President. We need to get you out of here now. The Russians are planning to fire another missile on Washington."

Reynolds's staffers grabbed him and dragged him through the hallways of the White House. They arrived at a large metal door and twisted it open. It moaned as it unveiled a dark stairwell down into a bunker. Reynolds hurried down the stairs and turned back, realizing he heard no other steps behind him. His staffers all stood at the top of the stairs.

"Don't worry, Mr. President. We will take care of things up here. Secret Service agents are waiting for you in the bunker."

"But you'll die!" Reynolds yelled up.

The woman nodded and shut the door. It twisted into a locked position. Reynolds followed overhead lights into a conference room with the presidential seal on the wall. Flat screen TVs played news of the attack. Nobody was waiting for him. The phone line was cut.

"What the hell?" Reynolds said, searching around the room for signs of life. He sat at the head of the table and rubbed his face. When he removed his hands, someone was sitting at the other end of the table. An old, Native American man with a light shining from the center of his chest. Braids hung down on either side of the light and were entrancing. His face was painted with black designs in sharp angles.

"This is how it will end if you proceed, Richard Reynolds," the man said. "Your own country will not trust you in a time of great crisis. You will be trapped here, in a prison of your own making."

"Trapped? The fuck you talking about? I'm the goddamn president! They can't do this to me!" Reynolds banged his fist on the table. It felt like a mattress when he struck it. *Weird.*

"When you wake, you must not take your political career any further," the man said, standing to leave the room. His body now seemed translucent. "You will bring far too much pain to innocent people. Bask in your unearned riches and walk away, Richard Reynolds, or burn in the fire you started."

An explosion of heat enveloped the room as the head of a missile burst through the ceiling. Reynolds felt his entire body burn and watched his skin slough off the bone. He wiggled his fingers—only bones—and screamed in agony. He burned for what felt like hours until he woke up in the hospital. He was sitting up in the arms of a doctor.

"Mr. Reynolds, are you alright?" he asked.

Reynolds's entire body shook. Sweat caused his gown to cling to his chest. His breath slowed as he got his bearings. He examined his hands, which were fully intact. Morning light came through the window of his room as he sat back.

"We thought we'd lost you there for a second," the doctor admitted with a chuckle. Reynolds, delirious, thought his behavior was unprofessional. "You've been in a coma for a week, Mr. Reynolds. I just came in for our regular check-in and here you are, screaming something fierce. Any dreams you'd like to share?"

Reynolds glared at the doctor, who had a soul patch at the bottom of his stupid face.

"No," Reynolds said. "Can I get some fucking water?"

"Yes. One sec." The doctor hurried over to the sink and filled a glass. He handed it to Reynolds, who gulped it down.

"What happened to the bastard who shot me?"

"Oh, I forgot you haven't been able to keep up with everything. They arrested him, Mr. Reynolds. He's in jail awaiting trial."

Reynolds set the glass on the nightstand to his right. "Pfft... Trial. Just hang the motherfucker."

"It's been all over the news, Mr. Reynolds. You're something of a hero. Everyone has been rooting for you to pull through, and there's been quite a bit of pressure on our medical team. I'm just relieved to see you alive and acting like yourself."

Reynolds glared at him. "You don't seem like a doctor. No offense."

"No, it's okay. Mr. Hardy sent me. Chuck. From New York? I'm the one who typically performs surgery on some of the guys up there if they get into trouble. He insisted I fly down here and work on you, so here I am."

Reynolds wondered why Chuck would send a doctor who seemed so… green; so annoyingly conversational.

"Are you somebody's kid?" Reynolds asked.

"Yeah, actually. Chuck's my uncle. His youngest brother is my old man. We live in North Jersey but we see Uncle Chuck all the time. It's funny, they have this hilarious relationship where…"

"Stop. Shut up. Sorry kid, I really don't give a dusty fuck about your family. Just call Chuck and tell him thanks, alright?"

"Will do, Mr. Reynolds."

"Great. And when the hell can I get out of here?"

"About a week or so now that you're up. But you'll have to take it easy."

"Yeah. Right. Get Oleg on the phone, too, will you? Tell him to come down here."

The doctor nodded and shut the door behind him. Reynolds sank back onto his pillow and groped for the TV remote on the table. He flipped it to the news.

"Thanks, Ashley," a female reporter said, standing outside the hospital. "No word yet on the condition of Las Vegas businessman and mayoral candidate Richard Reynolds who was shot early last week by a radical protestor named Andre Gibson. Gibson, of course, has a rap sheet filled with petty crimes along with an armed robbery charge a few years back, and he was part of a group that rejected Reynolds's candidacy. The assassination attempt has created a significant national following for the Las Vegas mayoral race, with thousands rallying online in support of Reynolds and many more sending in donations to his campaign. If Reynolds wakes from his coma and chooses to campaign again, he has the inside track to the job after this incident, Ashley."

Click. Reynolds turned off the TV and smiled. His chest was sore as he pushed himself up to a seated position. He took another sip of water and stared out the window. Beyond a nearby golf course, he saw the tip of the stratosphere and the flashing lights of the Strip. This would be his city soon enough, he thought, but did he really want that?

18

THE TIRES SCREECHED ON THE pavement as Daniel sped out of the parking lot. Gabby pressed her hands against the ceiling of the car to maintain balance. Tension gripped Daniel's forearms.

"Daniel, slow down! We're fine," Gabby said.

He squeezed the steering wheel, turning his knuckles white. "Hand me your cell phone."

"What?"

"Just give it to me. I need to make a call."

Gabby searched her bag and pulled out her phone. Daniel ripped it from her hands and dialed, rapidly switching his glance from the road to the keypad. He pressed the phone to his ear and waited for Gus to answer. Finally, he picked up.

"Hello, who is calling? You aren't on the approved list. I'm gonna hang up."

"Gus, it's Daniel. I'm calling from someone else's phone. I need a stow and go, ASAP. I'm going to be there in 10 minutes tops."

"Okay, Daniel, no worries. Car might not be ready right away, but I'll open the gate for you now."

"Alright, thanks, Gus. See you soon."

Click.

Daniel pressed his foot on the gas pedal, and the engine revved. He ran a red light but darted his head around to search for any potential police officers. He worried about Reynolds's men coming after him, too, but no cars appeared to be trailing them, yet.

"Daniel, this is fucking crazy. Nobody is following us. Slow down."

"We can't be sure of that, Gabby. This is Reynolds we're talking about."

"Reynolds is dead! You saw Andre shoot him, right? With how old he is, there's no way he survives two bullets to the chest."

"I've got a bad feeling, alright? Call it an inkling or some paranormal shit or whatever, but I really don't think Andre got him. A head shot? That's a different story. But it still feels like…"

"Feels like what?"

"I don't know. This anxiety in my stomach I've been feeling since Sarah was killed—it hasn't gone away. There's no relief."

Gabby's brow furrowed. "Have you considered that you might just be experiencing post-traumatic stress from witnessing an assassination? And not knowing what happened to Andre? Oh, and I almost forgot, you helped Jennifer drag her father's dead body to a pickup truck after he had a massive heart attack?"

Sweat ran along Daniel's temple. Gabby was right. Today was another in a growing list of clusterfucks. But he'd seen his fair share of bloodshed before. What was different about this? Still, the thought lingered in his mind that the Wendigo was still out there and that Reynolds wasn't quite dead yet. He thought about Reynolds's cane tapping on marble. The security video of him squatting down and tasting blood was stuck in Daniel's memory.

Andre was fine, right? He'd seemed to have everything under control for someone who had a 400-pound security guard on top of him, last Daniel checked. He was smiling, too. Impossible to forget that shit-eating grin. They probably had Andre tied to a chair in some warehouse, just like Daniel had been not too many nights ago. Would he find a way to escape, or would he talk his way into a shallow grave?

"Daniel!" Gabby yelled, grabbing the steering wheel and pulling it toward her. The car narrowly veered out of the way of an oncoming semi-truck. Its horn blared in Daniel's ears as he regained awareness. He almost missed the turn toward Gus's auto shop.

"Shit! I'm sorry." He rubbed his eyes and focused on the road.

"Should I drive?"

"No, I'm fine. We're almost there."

Sure enough, Gus had left the gate open for Daniel to swing it wide and pull in without a trace. The garage door closed behind the car, and Gus arrived at his window. Daniel rolled it down.

"No bullet holes this time, eh?" Gus said with a chuckle. "Why you in such a hurry, my boy? And where is your shirt?"

"Might have someone after us," Daniel replied, looking down at his chest. "And it's a long story. Thanks for this, Gus. We should be good now: didn't see any trail for the last mile or so."

"No problem. If you wanna hang out in the old waiting room, I'll prep you a new vehicle."

Daniel got out and met Gabby outside her door. She hugged him up around his shoulders. Out of some primal desire, he wanted to pick her up and kiss her against the wall, but he just returned the hug and led her to the waiting room. Through a creaking glass door, they stepped on cracked linoleum floors. A fluorescent light flickered above them. Dust and cobwebs littered the floor along with discarded cigarettes and dirty footprints.

Daniel and Gabby sat in the aging chairs near a coffee table. Magazines from decades ago were scattered across its surface. Daniel had the urge to pick one up and read it to quell his anxiety with something distracting, but instead, he held Gabby close.

"What are we going to do?" she asked.

"I just realized I need to make another call. Stay here."

"What, with the rats?"

Daniel got up and headed for the door. He turned back and smiled. "There are no rats. At least, I don't think so. I'll ask Gus when I talk to him."

"Gee, thanks."

Daniel let the door swing shut behind him and went outside to meet Gus, who was cleaning out a junk car for him.

"Won't be too long now, Daniel. Just got to get this presentable for your lady friend. Another new one, huh?"

"She's an old one, actually. The other one, well, she's… she's gone."

Gus looked at Daniel like a concerned father. He stopped what he was doing and put his hand on Daniel's shoulder.

"Sorry to hear that. Always fish in the sea, ain't that right?"

"Right. So, Gus, do you still have that old payphone on the property?"

"Yep. Right around the corner over there by the dumpster. You need coins?"

"Yeah, I do. Sorry. I'll pay you back."

"It's no bother. You and Andre pay me well enough. Speaking of, where is that *cabrón*?"

"He's in some trouble," Daniel said, taking the coins from Gus's rough palm. "I don't know where he is."

Gus shook his head. "Well, wherever he is, he'll be alright. He's a smart kid, like you."

"Certain kind of smart, I guess," Daniel said as he turned his back and headed for the payphone. He passed the dumpster and squeezed himself into the small phonebooth, inserted the coins and dialed. A whispering voice came through the phone.

"Hello? Who is this?"

"Oleg, it's Daniel. Are you alone?"

"Not quite," Oleg whispered. "Let me step outside real quick."

The tap of footsteps and turning of a doorknob preceded Oleg's return to the conversation.

"Okay," he said. "I'm alone. Just why the hell are you calling me right now? Do you have any idea what's going on?"

"I know, I know. I was there."

"You were there? What the fuck? You were with all those Indians?"

"Yes. And the guy who shot Reynolds was my friend Andre."

A long sigh from the other end of the line. Daniel worried Oleg might hang up. After all the time he'd spent carefully re-cruiting an informant inside Reynolds's organization, it felt like it was about to fall apart. Like everything else.

"Well, I can tell you that Reynolds is alive. Barely. They're operating on him now. Your friend got arrested. LVPD showed up too fast for our guys to figure out where to take him. They handcuffed him while he was unconscious."

"Jesus," Daniel said, rubbing his forehead. "Do you have any idea where Andre is now?"

"I assume they're holding him at the county jail, but you and I both know it's way too hot for you to come back to town right now. And I shouldn't even be talking to you. What if someone overhears this?"

"Who? Reynolds? Last you told me he's not exactly capable of listening to us right now." Daniel thought about the Wendigo. *Could it be listening?*

"You're right," Oleg said. "So, what is your next move?"

"I need you to confirm Andre's location. And keep me updated on Reynolds if you can."

"Okay… And how am I supposed to give you an update? Call some random payphone?"

"I'm gonna give you a number. Can you memorize it?"

"Yeah, sure, whatever."

Daniel gave him Gabby's cell phone number with instructions to call him at 6 a.m. the next day. He banged the payphone against its holder, and a few coins fell out. He jammed them in his pocket and went to check on Gabby.

She was on her phone, laughing at some video. *Anything to cope, I guess.*

"Babe," he said, not realizing until after the word left his lips how inappropriate it was. "You ready to go?"

She grimaced. "Oh, Daniel, please don't call me that. I know you're hurting but please, can we not do this?"

"Sorry… Old habit. Car's waiting. You ready?"

"Yes," she said, hurrying to join him on a stroll to their new ride. Gus was waiting with the keys. He handed them to Daniel with a slap on the back.

"Now," Gus said. "I don't want to see you back here again for a while now, okay? I don't need whatever heat you're bringing around town."

"Got it," Daniel replied. "Thanks for this, Gus. We owe you big time."

"No shit," Gus said with a laugh, waving them off as Daniel shut the door. Déjà vu kicked in for Daniel when the engine struggled to start. *My knights in shining armor*, Sarah had said. But armor made them slow. They weren't fast enough to save her from the monster under the proverbial bridge; the monster from the painting, from the safehouse, and who knows where else.

They hit the road and sat in silence. Gabby's sudden touch made Daniel flinch. She rubbed his arm to try and relax him, but the tension still hadn't left his body. He needed sleep, but he feared it. If there was ever a night for the Wendigo to visit him again, tonight seemed like a logical one. He was suffering, and it fed off that, right? That's what Soaring Eagle had said.

Soaring Eagle. Daniel had been so wrapped up with Andre's situation that he—like Gabby had earlier—briefly forgot about the horror the old man endured. The stress of the moment must have given him a heart attack, Daniel thought, but his eyes looked... petrified. Daniel glanced down at the splotches of paint remaining on his chest and wondered if Soaring Eagle's death was somehow caused by the Wendigo. Before, he wasn't sure how much he believed in the legend, but recent events had him questioning everything.

After a quiet ride to Henderson, they pulled into the driveway of the safehouse. Daniel locked the car and arrived at the porch, half-expecting the door to be wide open again. To his relief, it was shut, and the key was right under the shingle where it was supposed to be. When they entered the living room and turned into the kitchen, a knife sat idly on the counter, and the bullet-scarred milk carton remained in the sink. Everything was as he'd left it: haphazard and borderline unexplainable.

"Let's go get cleaned up," Gabby said.

Daniel followed Gabby upstairs to the bathroom where they disrobed as she turned on the shower. Cold water spewed from the rickety showerhead and didn't appear to warm up, even as Gabby turned the dial all the way to H.

"We're gonna have to brave it," Daniel said, remembering Sarah's complaint about the hot water. His stomach clenched. "No hot water right now."

Gabby rolled her eyes and let her hair down. They got in together and danced around for a moment, laughing in reaction to the frigid spray. Gabby reached for the body wash and began scrubbing the paint off Daniel's chest. Daniel noticed that the cold water caused her nipples to perk up.

"Look up," she said. He obliged. She reached up and rubbed the underside of his chin and neck, taking care of the last of the paint.

"My turn," she said, reaching for the body wash. Daniel grabbed her arm and stopped her. He poured out some soap on his hands and caressed her body, cleaning the paint on her shoulders and down her neckline, then squatting down to wash off the remainder along her stomach and around her lower back. Daniel turned up and made eye contact with her. He picked Gabby up by the small of her back. They made love in the shower until the cold blast of the water got to be too much to bear. They laughed and left the stall to complete their activity with Gabby propped up on the bathroom counter. When they were done, they dried off, sweat and water droplets indistinguishable on their bodies.

They ended up in Daniel's bed, her in an oversized T-shirt and panties, he in only boxers. They stared out the window together at a clear night sky, glittering with stars. As clarity returned to Daniel's mind, so did an overwhelming sense of dread.

19

G ABBY'S PHONE BUZZED ON THE nightstand. It had been a week since Daniel had heard from Oleg, and he had a feeling this was him. Daniel smacked his dry lips and wiped drool from his face. He reached over her to grab the phone and press it to his cheek.

"Hello?" he whispered.

"Daniel. It's Oleg. Just wanted to give you a few updates."

"Yeah? What's up?"

"Andre is at the county jail; they have him under increased security. As I'm sure you already know, Reynolds has a bunch of cops in town on his payroll. They were instructed by higher ups in the organization to keep watch over Andre until Reynolds wakes up. And…"

"And?"

"He woke up this morning."

A chill started at the base of Daniel's skull and ran down his back. "Have you seen him? Is he…"

"He's totally lucid. Still not 100 percent physically, but the doctors say he can leave here in a week. I'm looking in at him now. He's in his room sleeping."

Anger bubbled in Daniel's stomach. "So why don't you just go in there and smother him with his pillow?"

Oleg laughed. "Yeah, okay, and dig myself an early grave? He's still my boss, Daniel, despite what we've got going on here."

"Right," Daniel said with a sigh. "Wishful thinking, I guess."

"What are you going to do next?"

"Not sure. I think I'm gonna head up north to the reservation today. No use trying to bust into a heavily guarded jail by myself. This isn't the Old West, and I'm fresh out of dynamite."

"Fair enough," Oleg said through a warm chuckle. "Andre should be fine. For now. Just figure out what you're going to do next. Reynolds wants revenge on your buddy, and he hasn't decided what to do yet."

"I'll think of something. Talk to you later, Oleg."

Gabby's eyes opened to Daniel leaning over her, putting her phone back on the nightstand. They widened.

"What the hell are you doing on my phone?" she asked.

"Just business," he said, falling back onto his pillow. "Checking in on Andre. He's in jail. Reynolds is alive—in a coma."

"He's alive? Jesus. That Wendigo thing must be keeping him from dying."

"Maybe. Speaking of death, I need to head up to the reservation today and pay my respects. We wouldn't have any clue what's going on without Soaring Eagle. Jennifer's gotta be devastated."

Gabby ran her hand across Daniel's chest. "Go without me. I don't need to get in your way."

Daniel sat up. "You're not in my way. I'd be losing my shit right now if it weren't for you. But it *is* better that you stay here. I'll leave a gun downstairs on the counter in case you need it."

"Ha! Yeah, right. I'll just utilize all that secret agent training they provided at art school. Take your damn gun. I feel safe enough here. And I've gotta work later, anyway."

Daniel nodded. He pecked Gabby on the cheek, got dressed, and left. He zoned out for the entire ride to the reservation, no music on the speakers. His mind wandered to dark places, thinking it might be better for everyone if he drove off the road into a tree. Depression clung to him, and he struggled to focus on the road. He took a sick pleasure in letting his thoughts drift into self-loathing, like he deserved this; like, no matter what happened, the world would be the same fucked-up place whether he was in it or not. And that if he'd done just one or two things differently, the people unlucky enough to have gotten wrapped up in his life would still be alive and far away from him.

The car came to a halt outside Jennifer's home, where flowers and gifts lined the front porch. Teddy bears, paintings, floral arrangements, and handwritten notes were stacked all around the entrance. Daniel got out and approached the door, knocking twice and waiting for what felt like forever. Finally, Jennifer's wife—*What's her name? Sandy!*—answered.

"Who are you?"

"I'm so sorry to intrude, Sandy. I'm Daniel, a friend of Jennifer's. I need to see her."

"She's not here. Can I tell her you dropped by?"

Daniel sighed. "I'm sorry, but it's urgent. Where can I find her?"

Sandy's face tightened with concern. She stepped outside, led Daniel to the edge of the porch and pointed.

"Her father's house is that way. Do you have a horse?"

"Do I have a horse? I've been there by car before, was just there last night. Is there some rule about no cars?"

"There was but… never mind," she said, putting a hand on his shoulder. "You be careful, and don't get my wife into anything dangerous. She's in pain and the questions she's asking herself aren't going to be answered with that gun on your hip."

Daniel noticed the weapon on his belt, embarrassed. "Sorry about this. I'm sure you're getting tired of your wife hanging around guys like me."

Sandy turned away. She appeared to be holding back tears.

"It's not your fault. Jennifer's always mixed with strange characters, no offense. She thinks she can help everybody, and I'm sure it's killing her that she couldn't help her dad."

Daniel shook his head. "Soaring Eagle was a great man. I only spent a night with the guy, but I feel like I've known him forever in a weird way."

"I know the feeling. A lot of folks in our tribe feel the same. He had a way, you know? He left an impression."

"No doubt. Well, I'm gonna head up to Jennifer. Thank you, Sandy."

"Sure," she replied, giving Daniel a hug before heading back inside. Daniel got back in his car and took a deep breath. He turned the keys and whipped the steering wheel to cruise through the desert toward Soaring Eagle's place.

Daniel slammed his car door shut and squinted up at the sky. It was hotter than he expected. The sun glared over the desert. A large bird flew overhead and eclipsed the sun with its wings for a moment, catching Daniel's attention. It dove lower and weaved gracefully through the wind. Daniel unhooked his holster from his belt and put it underneath the backseat of the car. With a turn of the key in the driver's side door, it was locked.

Daniel shielded his eyes from the sun and observed the bird as it soared. Its flight path led his eyes to a towering red rock near Soaring Eagle's former home. A figure stood on one of the ledges, looking out at the horizon. As Daniel got closer, sweat beading on his brow, he realized the figure was Jennifer.

He approached her with care. Soaring Eagle's daughter was sitting with her legs crossed and in some form of meditation. Daniel hesitated before tapping her on the shoulder.

"Uh… Jennifer? It's Daniel."

Jennifer's eyes opened slowly—they were bloodshot—and she forced a half-smile. "Hey, man. Have a seat."

Daniel lowered himself to the ground next to Jennifer. Pressing his hands on the warm rocks, he felt his tension ease.

"Now close your eyes and meditate with me, Daniel. It's what my dad would've wanted."

No conversation, huh? Just meditation?

Obliging the grieving woman's request, Daniel sat with his legs crossed and closed his eyes.

"Now, breathe slowly. In through your nose, hold it for a second, then out through your mouth."

In, out. In, out. Daniel felt the ends of his toes start to tingle and shifted in his spot. He kept going, though, and the numbness carried up his legs. He thought he was having a panic attack at first, or overheating, but his mindset grew calmer. After a few minutes of repetition, he opened his eyes. It was nighttime (*What the hell?*), and Jennifer was nowhere to be found. Daniel panicked until he was distracted by fire in the valley below.

Anger filled his chest as he watched teepees burn and heard women and children crying out. Upon closer examination, a group of White men in old clothes with rifles were terrorizing a group of Paiutes. Two of them were dragging a woman by the hair into one of the teepees they hadn't burned yet. She struggled and fought back, filling the air with her cries of terror.

Standing at the center of the lineup of horses was the Wendigo, its massive hand on the shoulder of one of the White men: the leading White man. He was barking orders at his troops while the Wendigo stood, motionless, smiling at the horrors before it. Daniel turned to his right and saw a rifle leaning against a tree. He grabbed it, aimed, and fired off the cliff toward the Wendigo. He missed.

The Wendigo's eyes darted up to the clifftop. It turned its host's head toward Daniel and pointed. The man directed his soldiers to fire on the cliff as a smile formed on the Wendigo's crooked face. Its yellow eyes glowed brighter. Daniel felt the sting of a bullet to the chest.

After blinking a few times, the pain went away, and he realized he'd returned to reality. Jennifer was sitting next to him, appearing concerned.

"Daniel, are you okay?"

"Yes... No... What was that?"

"You were supposed to see this. The group of White men slaughtering our people, right? That was hundreds of years ago. And the Wendigo was there."

Daniel gathered his thoughts and searched for danger. He felt his chest for a wound. Nothing. "But it felt real."

"This place, my father used to come here almost every day. He'd meditate, get in touch with his thoughts, see into the past and future. That is what we're here to do, why you wanted to come visit me today. It's supposed to feel real."

"I just... No, Jennifer. I came to see you to talk about your dad, help you through it. I didn't know we were gonna..."

"Have visions?" she smirked. "My dad wasn't the only one with this ability. We all have it, to a certain extent. Most of us just don't tap into it. You have déjà vu sometimes, right?"

"Yeah, of course. Everyone does."

"Well, that's part of it. Things people call instinct or intuition, that's part of it, too. This isn't just some magical Indian mumbo jumbo. White folks have it, Black folks, Asian folks, Native folks like me, everybody. Some people tap into this ability more than others, even without knowing it."

"So today, my coming here, that was me using this… ability your father had?"

"You bet. And my dad made sure of that. Before you got here, I spoke to him in one of these visions. He said he'd provide you a guiding light; take you under his wing."

Daniel thought about the bird he saw earlier. *An eagle?*

"This is a lot to take in, Jennifer. What am I supposed to do with all of this? And how am I supposed to know you didn't slip me some peyote or something?"

Jennifer cackled. "I didn't drug you, man. What you're seeing now and what you just saw during meditation, they're both real. These visions, they serve a purpose. My father was killed by the Wendigo, but he said his death will help us get rid of it. He always used to say that everyone has a role to play in the universe's grand design. That's some seriously cryptic shit for your average person to wrap their head around, but you have to think through that lens if you're going to interpret what you saw."

Daniel paused. He scratched his head. "I saw the Wendigo in that vision. It was forcing those military guys to kill Native people. *Your* people."

"That's right," Jennifer said, pushing herself up into a standing position. She extended a hand to Daniel and lifted him up. "'Ours is a history painted in blood and suffering.' Another one of my dad's famous lines. He'd say shit like that to me as a kid, and I didn't know what he meant until now. He wasn't just talking about Paiutes or Native people in general. The history of humanity is one of violence, of suffering, always at the hands of the powerful, greedy, or corrupted. This time with Reynolds is no different."

Daniel brushed the dust off his pants. "He's alive, you know."

"I know."

Daniel raised an eyebrow. "How could you possibly know that? Your dad tell you that, too?"

Jennifer smiled. "Nope. That's just instinct. From what my dad taught me about the Wendigo, it makes sure its hosts don't drop dead too soon. It has a plan for everything. It lingers. There's no killing it, at least not outright. There are ways to get rid of it, but it always comes back, especially if you don't execute the old rituals properly."

Daniel coughed. The dry air was getting to him; he needed water. "Well, that's depressing. So, what are we supposed to do?"

"Right now? Nothing. We've just got to hope Reynolds loses that election. We can work with Christina on getting out the vote against him, but it's an uphill battle after what Andre did. Reynolds has become a kind of cult hero for the worst parts of the Internet. I saw on the news this morning that a bunch of extremists are rallying behind him online."

Daniel's stomach lurched. He was disgusted. Or was he just hungry?

"I don't want to speak for her, but Gabby and I are willing to help however we can in the next few months. With all the heat around what happened, I think it's better that I lie low for a while and work behind the scenes. Rough way to start a career in politics."

Jennifer laughed and put a strong arm around Daniel, who felt like he'd gained a new friend out of all this tragedy; a stand-in for Andre while he was in the clink, but with far fewer tendencies for lewd humor and sexual innuendo. He felt hopeful with Jennifer in his corner, like they'd find a way to rescue Andre and escape all of this unscathed, all while putting an end to Reynolds's ambitions.

"There are worse ways to get involved in politics," Jennifer said. "Just look at Reynolds."

20

THE BED MADE ANDRE'S BACK ache. The toilet had no seat, and the toilet paper was too thin. But the worst part of being in jail was that he couldn't jerk off in peace. He hadn't jerked off at all, actually, in the week since he arrived. That only heightened his anxiety.

"Yo," he said to his cellmate Lenny, whose snoring could have rattled the windows (if there were any). The guy kept droning on until Andre raised his voice. "YO! Wake up!"

A vicious snort and Lenny was awake, turning his gaze across the room to Andre with weary eyes. "The fuck you want, man?"

"You're snorin', bro. Turn on your fuckin' side or some shit. I can't sleep."

Lenny rolled over and faced the wall. Andre stared up at the ceiling, hands folded on his chest, wondering how his life ended up here. Tomorrow would be eight days, by Andre's count, that he'd been locked up for killing Richard Reynolds. Nobody had spoken to him about the case, save for the state-appointed lawyer who just spoke in platitudes for half an hour. Even though Andre knew he was more than guilty of what they'd arrested him for, he still felt a sense of injustice, like no matter what he did, he couldn't get a fair shake.

He'd been locked up before. Petty shit: shoplifting, carrying an unlicensed weapon, drug possession. The kinds of things they hit you on when they're fishing for something else. This time felt different. It was like he was up a creek without a paddle, only he had to find a way upstream in a canoe littered with bullet holes.

Andre smiled thinking about the terror on Reynolds's face. He deserved it, the old prick. All those neo-Nazi motherfuckers probably held a candlelight vigil in his honor, then went back to their trailers and roasted up a raccoon for dinner. What he did wasn't just revenge for Sarah or a way of getting rid of the Wendigo. It was a message from the *real* working class to the people who sought to bring them down. Andre thought he should be paraded through the streets like the anti-capitalist hero he was, not locked up in this shithole.

The metal door into the cell block creaked open. A guard lumbered down the hallway and stopped near Andre's cell. Andre pretended to be asleep as he heard the footsteps approach.

"Gibson," the guard said. "You have a visitor."

Andre sat up in disbelief. *Dan?* "The fuck you mean I have a visitor? Ain't it like 1:30 in the morning?"

The guard, a portly White man with a handlebar mustache, glanced at his watch. "2:11, actually."

Andre waited as the guard unlocked the cell and escorted him out. Lenny snored through it all. *Dude probably wouldn't notice if a riot broke out.* He followed the guard through the tight hallways of the jail and into one of the interrogation rooms.

"I thought you said I was talkin' to a visitor," Andre queried.

"You are. He wanted to meet you in here. Now shut up and have a seat." The guard whapped Andre on the backside with his nightstick. It made him angry, but he held back and sank into the chair. A yellow light flickered in the lamp above the aging wooden table. Andre spread his dark fingers on the surface and tapped them while he waited. Something felt off about this entire situation. *Why would Dan want to meet me in here?*

A voice came across the guard's walkie-talkie. "He's here. Step out, Davis."

The security guard obliged, leaving Andre alone in the room. It was silent for a few minutes until an echo came down the hallway outside: heavy steps and the sound of rickety wheels rolling on concrete. The door creaked open and a large man in a dark suit backed in, pulling someone in a wheelchair into the room. The chair turned toward Andre, revealing its occupant.

"Hello there," Reynolds said. Andre's eyes widened. He stood to lunge at Reynolds but was met with a swift fist to the face. When he fell back in the chair and wiped the blood from his lip, he saw the punch had come from Reynolds's heavyset Black security guard from the rally.

"You've already met Tyson, haven't you, Andre?" Reynolds asked, wheeling himself up to the table. The light revealed his sunken, gaunt appearance. He was small and skinny after standing tall and broad-chested on that stage eight days ago; dark under his eyes like he hadn't slept in weeks.

Andre glared. "How the fuck you still alive? You took two slugs to the chest and you're old as fuck. Am I missin' somethin'?"

Reynolds snickered. "You aren't *missing* anything. In fact, you were the only one there to see the whole picture. Remember my tall friend? The red guy?"

The back of Andre's neck stung. He remembered the horror in Soaring Eagle's eyes as the Wendigo stood over him.

"You were the only one who could see him, Andre. Even I couldn't see what was really going on; he didn't want me to know what was coming. That's part of his—our—plan, you see. He's since explained to me that getting shot, while painful, was a necessary step for the advancement of my political career. The people fucking love me, Andre. Have you seen the news?"

Andre wanted to reach across the table and choke Reynolds out. He wasn't worried about another run-in with Tyson; he'd fought bigger guys before and come out clean on the other side. What he was really worried about was the Wendigo making an appearance.

"Is that thing—the Wendigo—in here with you?" he asked.

Reynolds laughed. "Wendigo? What, you gave it a name now? Here, let me ask him. Hey, buddy, is your name 'Wendigo'?"

Silence for a moment. Reynolds looked off to the corner of the room and nodded.

"He said that's what all the Indians used to call him back in the day. Said he hadn't run into those guys in a while… until their little escapade at my rally."

Andre watched Reynolds struggle to lift himself out of the wheelchair.

Tyson ran over to help. "Sir, Mr. Reynolds, you shouldn't be doin' this."

Reynolds slapped his hand away. "Get the fuck offa me. You want to end up like your soul brother over there with a fat lip? Keep trying to help me like I'm some kind of invalid."

Tyson backed away and left Reynolds alone. His wrinkled, convulsing hands pressed on the edge of the table as he brought himself to a standing position. He extended his right hand to Andre, pointing with force.

"Now, you listen close, Sambo. I could kill you right fucking here if I wanted to. My boys, they would've taken care of it if I gave the order. Shanked in the prison yard: that woulda been the end of old Andre Gibson. But it wasn't. You know how your story ends?"

Andre scoffed, sizing up the old man as he stood over him. "How exactly you gonna end it?"

Reynolds's face reddened. He flashed a smile as his eyes began to glow bright yellow. The lamp hanging over the table went out, filling the room with darkness, save for the light from Reynolds's eyeballs. The light flashed back on, and Reynolds banged his fist on the table, standing without the aid of his cane. Black veins pulsated in his neck and down his arms. When he flashed another grin, his teeth were rotten, sharp, filled with holes.

"What the fuck?" Andre backed away from the table, pressing against the wall.

"Your story ends in here, Andre Gibson," a deep, unnatural voice said from Reynolds's mouth. "It might not be from this crime or during this sentence, but you will die in a cell. Your arrogance will lead you down the same path so many of your people have gone down before. And the suffering you bring on yourselves has sustained me for many years."

Andre's fear turned to anger.

"You don't know shit about me. People like me don't bring this shit on ourselves. It's the damn system holding us down. You been around, what, thousands of years? And you don't see that?"

Reynolds's body shook with laughter. "Call it what you want—a system, 'the man,' oppression—you will end up here. You've failed, Andre, and that's a greater punishment than death for someone like you. Someone who doesn't fear death is prone to suffer while alive, and you've ensured suffering for more than just yourself."

Andre shook his head, sweat running down his face. He slid along the wall and backed away from Reynolds, who stalked him around the room like a big cat, walking with ease and leaving behind burn marks on the floor.

"When you first planned the robbery, I knew you would seek out the girl named Sarah. I sent the shooter to ambush you and your friends outside the hotel. It made you trust her, yes?

Showed she was up for this little job you were planning? You ended up feeding her to me on a silver platter when you sent her to that blackjack game."

Reynolds's tongue, forked and slimy, moistened his lips. One more cackle before he returned to the wheelchair, leaning back in relaxation. When he turned to Andre again, Reynolds's face and voice were back to normal.

"So, ya see, Andre, you played right into the hand you were dealt. You'll be found guilty of trying to kill me, of course, and you'll rot in here. Shoot, I might even have my lawyers make a push for the chair and save you from all this suffering we've been talking about. Because I'm so grateful for what you've done for me."

Reynolds rolled toward the door and signaled for Tyson to open it.

"So long for now, Andre. See you at the trial."

The door slammed shut as they departed, leaving Andre alone again. Andre sank to the floor and cried out with equal parts terror and anguish. He'd failed, and the price was worse than his life. Reynolds was going to use this to win the election and make life even harder for people like him and the people he cared about. And nothing could stop the Wendigo from getting what it wanted, either.

The security guard returned to the room and lifted Andre up off the floor. "Come on now. Back to your cell."

Andre walked, feeling numb, back to his cage. He sat on the edge of his bed as the guard slammed the bars shut, locking him in. Davis whistled while he left the cell block, not a care in the world, mindlessly serving The Man. Andre fell onto his pillow and let out a deep breath. Lenny snorted for air in the bed across the cell.

"Man," Andre said to himself. "I need to get the fuck up outta here."

21

I**T PISSED** R**EYNOLDS OFF THAT** Tyson had to lift him into the car. He could handle himself, no matter what that asshole doctor said about "taking it easy."

"There ya go," Tyson said, reaching for the seatbelt to strap Reynolds in. He slapped his hand away, *Second time I've had to do that* tonight, and glared at him.

"I can buckle my fucking self in," Reynolds said. His thoughts turned to his comatose hallucinations. "I'm not a child."

"My bad, Mr. Reynolds," Tyson replied. He slammed the door shut, and Reynolds buckled himself in. They drove back to The Luxury where Oleg was waiting outside the front door. He flashed a smile and waved as they pulled up.

Tyson set up the wheelchair outside the door and let Reynolds lower himself into it. Wheeling up to Oleg, Reynolds extended a hand. Oleg shook it.

"Good to see you again, boss. You look better."

"Feeling better, Oleg. How are things going with the public? They lapping it up that ol' Reynolds has returned to save the day?"

"News this morning was good. I had someone on your political staff tell them to stay off the property so you could have your privacy. We have the live stream all set up in your office for this afternoon."

"Perfect. How about job applications?"

"Thousands of them. From all over the state and some from around the country. There are letters too, boss. You've got a lot to read from people who are behind you."

Reynolds smiled. His arms got tired, so he motioned for to Tyson to push him the rest of the way to his personal elevator. What he didn't expect when they turned the corner was a crowd of his remaining hotel workers standing in the elevator bay, cheering and clapping as he approached. White, all of them, with the exception of a few Black guys who worked in the kitchen. He'd tolerate that, for now. He needed support from those guys, too, if he wanted to win the election.

"Oh, please," Reynolds said, raising his arms to the crowd. "Thank you all so much for your support. We're gonna keep putting you guys first!"

A concierge worker shook his hand and smiled big. It creeped Reynolds out; reminded him of the child who'd led him through the nightmare casino. A chill brushed across the back of Reynolds's neck as Tyson pushed him into the elevator. Tyson, Reynolds, and Oleg rode up to the apartment. When the doors slid open, Reynolds was relieved to be home. He ditched the wheelchair and grabbed a cane leaning against the wall near the entrance—his old one. It was a crutch for a bum foot before, but he really needed it now with how weak he felt from the surgery.

He sank into the couch and let out a deep breath. "Tyson, go on home, now. Oleg and I have some business to discuss."

"Sure thing, boss. Stay well and don't push it too hard."

Reynolds nodded. Tyson left. Oleg sat in the chair across from Reynolds and handed him a stiff drink on the rocks. More of that top-shelf booze from Chuck. Still smooth, but a bit irritating going down. *Must be leftover pain from the operation.*

"So," Oleg said. "What's the plan for this big live stream you had us set up? You have a speech ready? Want me to help write one?"

Reynolds scoffed. "You? Write? I don't wanna sound like Putin or Stalin here, Oleg, I'm a red-blooded American. I've got a few things in mind, but it'll be pretty quick. Just want the people to see my gorgeous mug—proof of life, above all else. Don't want 'em to think you guys are pullin' a *Weekend at Bernie's* on them."

Oleg laughed, though Reynolds didn't think it sounded genuine. He tabled his skepticism and leaned forward, setting his drink on the coaster in front of him.

"We're gonna win this thing, Oleg. I've got a feeling. With all the people getting behind me online and the way the media is acting like I'm some kind of martyr, it's perfect. I've wanted something like this for a long time. To be honest, I was getting sick of all the late nights and dark alleys. Think of how history will remember me now."

Oleg forced a smile. Reynolds's suspicions rang a tiny alarm in the back of his head. *Who is this guy trying to fool?*

"What was the other business you wanted to discuss?" Oleg asked.

Reynolds examined Oleg up and down. "Who's askin'?"

"Well, me, of course. What do you mean, boss?"

"I mean you're actin' funny… not yourself. There something you want to tell me?"

"No, I just…"

"Just what?" Reynolds's voice rose. "What the fuck are you hiding?"

"Nothing, boss. I just got word today that Andre Gibson's partner—Daniel, I think his name is—nobody can find him. I know you asked me to take some guys up to the reservation, but he's not there. We asked that doctor where he was, and she had no idea who we were talking about. He must have skipped town."

Reynolds cleared his throat. "Fuck him. He won't bother us again."

"Yes, he will," came the whisper.

Reynolds's body flinched.

"What, boss?" Oleg asked, concern on his face.

"Nothing. Just… leave me alone for a bit, alright? We can talk business some other time. I need to rest."

"Uhh… sure. No problem, boss. I'll get out of your hair."

Reynolds ignored him and bit his nails. After Oleg left, his body convulsed for a moment before black smoke billowed around his mouth. The beast appeared in the center of the room.

"You should be wary of this Daniel character," it said, taking lumbering steps toward the chair Oleg was previously sitting in. It sat and left burn marks in the leather with its jagged fingernails.

"Why? He's just some petty criminal, and he's alone now. Nobody left to back him up. Security around me is airtight, especially now."

The beast crossed one muscular red leg over the other. "You need to turn your mind to the future, Richard. What you seek is within your grasp, but I need you to want more."

"What does this have to do with that asshole Daniel?"

"He is a threat to what you seek. One that needs to be snuffed out. Your ambitions are changing, Richard. I can feel it."

Reynold searched his thoughts for what this thing was talking about. He saw the oval office again, as clearly as if it were right in front of him.

"President? Not me, man. Mayor of Vegas, local legend, protector of the real American worker, that all sounds nice. *That* is a legacy. But being president ain't for me. If you knew what I saw while I was under, you'd run like hell from this shit, too."

"I saw what you dreamed, you sniveling coward. I was there.

It was a hallucination—your mind playing tricks on you. If I could control it, I would've shown you something else."

Reynolds was skeptical of the beast now. How much control did it have over him, exactly?

"I thought you could help me see into the future. It got me here, right? You knew I'd get shot, and the bullet took the tumor right out of my lung. That ain't a fucking coincidence. That's some divine—err… demonic—intervention, right?"

The beast smiled. Its teeth always seemed disgusting to Reynolds. And that was coming from a guy whose teeth had yellowed from decades of cigarettes. He sure as shit could go for one right now, but that was a big no-no from the doctor.

"Yes, Richard, I directed those bullets to strike you in that way, and it is my influence that got you here in the first place. But the dreams you saw—of your failures, of the nuclear attack—those were not put there by me. Another entity, something with different intentions, infected your mind. Because you were weak. As we get stronger, he won't be able to weasel his way into the recesses of your mind."

"*He?*" Reynolds asked, standing up with aid of the cane. "Who do you mean? You killed that Indian. It isn't him, is it?"

The beast seemed confused, frustrated. It tossed the chair across the room in anger where it disintegrated into ash on the floor.

"I don't know."

"You don't know? So much for all knowing, huh?"

A puff of smoke and the beast was standing in front of him. It gripped his neck and held him up in the air.

"Let… me… go…" Reynolds choked.

"Listen to me, you cockroach. I will give you what you want, but you have to want the right thing for our path to go as planned. When you win this election, it will not be enough. I want *more.*"

Heat emanated from the beast's fingers and stung Reynolds's

neck. He wriggled and tried to fight out of its grasp, but the demon's grip tightened.

"If you aren't capable of giving me what I want, perhaps I should just kill you right here."

Reynolds shook his head in desperation. His windpipe was being crushed. He was drowning in his own blood. The beast's face grew closer to his. Heat came from its nostrils, its triangular face a horror show within inches of his eyes.

"You continue to disappoint me, Richard. I'm afraid that drastic measures are necessary for our mutual goals to be achieved."

Reynolds's eyes bugged out; he was losing consciousness. The tightness around his neck became too much to bear. He coughed and squirmed and shook until his body gave up. Everything went black.

His eyes opened again, but he was across the room, alone, watching his own death. The beast dropped his limp body on the couch, and Reynolds saw emptiness behind his corpse's eyes. He panicked and tried to run over and save himself, but he couldn't move: his feet were translucent and locked to the floor. *Am I a fucking ghost?*

The beast disappeared in a cloud of black smoke and entered Reynolds's body through the nostrils. The body shook violently, and the bruises around its neck disappeared. Twisted and slumped over the arm of the couch, its eyes opened, bright yellow. It blinked a few times, and the eyes became a version of normal, jaundiced a bit around the edges. Reynolds tried to make the horror stop, but he still couldn't move from his position across the room.

"Oh, Richard," his corporeal form said in the beast's deep voice, before twisting to a standing position and switching to Reynolds's cadence. "I'm sorry it had to be this way, but business is business."

Small hands gripped Reynolds's ankles. He turned down to see the rotten fingers of children clawing at his shoes. More of them appeared by the second. A child's laugh echoed in the back of his mind. It grew louder, joined by a chorus of little girls and boys cackling at his suffering. Their hands began to drag him through the floor, and he tried to kick them off, running down the hall toward his bedroom.

He fell facedown next to the bathroom. That girl—Sarah—was standing in front of the shower, wearing a bright red pant-suit. Her hair was up, and her eyes were missing. She laughed along with the children whose hands continued to grip and drag Reynolds across the floor. He felt his feet burn. The heat traveled up his legs as he sank into a hole in the floor. Pain constricted his stomach and chest. His heart (*Do I still have one?*) was beating faster and faster until it stopped. He was fully submerged and looked up through the hole in the floor: blackness engulfing him as the children's nails dug into his skin. He screamed, but no noise came out of his mouth. He saw his own face, grinning, peering down the hole with rotten teeth and yellow eyes. It waved goodbye.

22

DANIEL SAT ON A BENCH on the Strip, gazing up at the glittering lights of the casinos towering over him. It had been four months since the election. He looked down at the sidewalk and saw a small card with a topless blonde woman on it, the name *BRANDY* in purple letters below a photo of her squeezing her breasts together—bulbous, silicone monstrosities.

Daniel picked the card up and examined it. There was a phone number on the back to call for Brandy. He considered dialing. Gabby hadn't spoken to him in a few weeks after their latest blowout, and he figured this might finally be it. Saving himself from a night of disappointment paired with heavy financial losses, he tossed Brandy's card aside and walked away.

Pulling a cigarette out of his pocket and popping it in his mouth, Daniel shielded it from the wind with one hand and sparked it up with the other. The hot sting reached the back of his throat, and he puffed smoke into the cold Vegas night. Winter in the desert was comfortable during the day but especially crisp after 7 p.m. Daniel preferred this weather. He'd rather have his hands clinging to warmth inside his jacket pockets than to be sweating from neck to balls.

A homeless family caught Daniel's eyes as he strolled past Caesar's Palace. In the past, homeless people rode solo along the streets, but he was seeing more and more of this since Reynolds won: husbands and wives with their children in tow, once reliant on jobs in the service industry before being forced into degradation. The anti-immigrant policies Reynolds touted on his campaign trail went into effect quickly with minimal opposition from the state legislators he'd paid off. Corruption infected every layer of local government, and the people who were duped into pulling the lever for Reynolds on election day were no better off today than four months ago. Still, they worshipped him.

Reynolds ran his city government like the mob: self-serving and inflicting suffering on those who dared to challenge his criminal syndicate. Suffering he likely didn't give a shit about, as long as he looked good. His speeches had somehow become angrier since he won, like he wasn't satisfied with the pain he'd caused in such a short time. He wanted more.

Daniel pulled a pair of $20 bills from his wallet and handed them to the family. They nodded and smiled up at him but didn't say anything. Behind glassy eyes, years of discrimination and being treated as less than had culminated in this moment of despondence. The little boy was crying. His older sister tried to calm him. Their mother shook in the cold, trying to stay warm under her husband's coat.

Anger built in Daniel's stomach. Before all this, he didn't give a shit about politics. He was worried about where he and Andre would rip someone off next, what their future scores would look like, how he would find a way out of this city. The shock value of Sarah's death, then Soaring Eagle's, woke something up inside him, something Daniel had never tapped into: a desire to help people. He'd been so focused on self-enrichment for most of his life that he didn't realize how similar he was to people like Reynolds, contributing to the struggles of those he intimidated.

All it took was one failed robbery to realize how wrong-minded he had been for so long. But how would he make up for the pain he'd caused in the years before he encountered Reynolds?

Daniel arrived at The Mirage with extra speed in his step. He was growing impatient, waiting for the moment his newest plan—a better plan—would come to fruition. He had a meeting scheduled with Jennifer to discuss the first step and meditate. So far, in their attempts, he hadn't been able to make contact with Soaring Eagle during meditation.

Jennifer planned a rendezvous in room 423, where Daniel had been spending much of his time since the election, self-medicating and whoring around behind Gabby's back. Daniel regretted his actions, but it was too late now.

Flashing his keycard over the door handle, the light turned green, and Daniel let himself in. Jennifer was sitting in a chair by the window, smoking out of a pipe. It was pretty badass, Daniel thought. For a moment, she appeared like a younger version of Soaring Eagle.

"What's up, Daniel?" Jennifer asked, setting the pipe on the ashtray next to her. She stood and gave Daniel a quick hug, and the pair sank into chairs on either side of the table by the window. The dark carpeting hid the stains of nights Daniel wished he could forget.

"This room's getting a little smelly, man." Jennifer waved her hand in front of her nose and laughed. "What the hell you been getting into?"

Daniel ignored the question. "Is everything set for tomorrow?"

"Yeah. Christina rounded up some of the troops to create a distraction, and you'll have a small window to break through the crowd and get him."

"Once I get Andre out of there, I need you to be ready with

the car running. You remember where we need you to park, right?"

"Yep. No problem."

Daniel was worried about all the factors at play and if his plan would even come close to working. But this was his only shot. He needed Andre for what was next, and he figured his best friend was struggling in isolation. The two had been inseparable since they were kids, and Daniel had been engaging in self-loathing and erratic behavior as of late without Andre by his side. Above all else, Andre kept Daniel grounded, focused on better-ing himself—even if Andre was sometimes a hypocrite.

"I'm gonna have one chance at this," Daniel said. "If he's with more than two officers, I'm probably fucked. But Oleg tells me they're parading him into the courthouse with an officer on each arm, just for the political stunt. Reynolds wants a show. He kept telling Oleg he wanted Andre to suffer."

Jennifer shook her head. "'Absolute power corrupts absolutely.'"

Daniel shot a sly look Jennifer's way. "You're turning into your old man with all these deep quotes."

"Ha! Yeah, right. I feel more like him every day. I think being a parent has allowed me to understand his perspective better."

"I'd say the visions and spiritual visits from beyond the grave probably have something to do with that, too," Daniel said with a laugh.

"Oh, you're definitely right. Speaking of, we should try and chat with him right now. Last time we talked, he said he had some important info for ya. 'Urgent business,' he called it."

"Alright," Daniel said. "But every time we do this I struggle to focus. And I haven't even seen him yet. Any advice?"

"Like I always tell you: it's all a matter of mindset. If you're not in the right headspace, you won't be able to reach him. Come over here."

Daniel followed Jennifer to the center of the room where they sat cross-legged on the floor, facing each other. They joined hands and began the traditional deep breathing while Jennifer spoke in her ancestors' tongue. When Daniel opened his eyes, it was silent. He was alone in a dark room, sitting at a wooden table with a flickering yellow light hanging above it. This was a first for their meditation sessions. A whisper from behind caused him to whip his head around. When he turned back, Soaring Eagle was sitting across from him.

"Hello, Daniel," Soaring Eagle said. "It has been a while, my friend."

Daniel smiled. "Good to see you. This isn't some mind trick, is it?"

"No," Soaring Eagle said. "This is me you're talking to. No tricks, just us."

Daniel paused, noticing he was free of anxiety in whatever dimension they were in. He sat forward and folded his hands on the table.

"Jennifer said you had something important to discuss with me."

"Yes. Before you embark on this journey to rescue Andre, I need to inform you of the true dangers you face."

Daniel gulped. "Like…?"

Soaring Eagle shifted in his seat. He seemed younger, stronger, with black paint in sharp, knife-like patterns on his face. There was a seriousness—even more so than usual—in his tone.

"Many months ago in your time, before what is left of Richard Reynolds became mayor, I visited him during his coma. After the shooting. Soon after my death."

Daniel looked away, distracted by more whispers, but Soaring Eagle grabbed his face and turned it toward his own.

"I tried to stop what has happened," Soaring Eagle said. "I showed Reynolds his future, what would happen if he kept satisfying his political ambition: suffering, scores dead, well beyond Las Vegas. I thought it would be enough to stop the Wendigo from achieving its goal. But I underestimated how powerful it had already become."

"Wha-what do you mean? It didn't work?"

"No. Reynolds was hesitant to do anything beyond running for mayor, and the Wendigo killed him. Sent his spirit to the underworld. The Reynolds you see now is merely a façade: the Wendigo disguising itself in his body."

Daniel felt like he was slipping out of the vision. Invisible hands seemed to be gripping his arms and dragging him out of the chair.

"So, how the hell do we stop it?"

"I have spoken to those who came before us. Those who share in my ability to see beyond the confines of the mortal world. They say a silver blade plunged into the heart will bring the Wendigo to heel. Burning the heart after removal is the only way to ensure it doesn't come back."

The distant whispering became an overwhelming chatter, then laughter and playful shrieking from what sounded like children. Soaring Eagle's face sank. He seemed worried, disappointed. *Why?* Daniel figured he only had a few more seconds before the hands dragged him away.

"There is one more thing," Soaring Eagle said. "This will be the last time you and I see each other. This is your journey now, Daniel, and I can only help you to a certain point. Your decisions from here on out will shape the future."

Soaring Eagle grabbed Daniel's hand and smiled behind tears. White light filled Daniel's field of vision and he woke up on the hotel floor, staring up at the ceiling fan. Jennifer ran over and helped him up.

"You good?" she asked.

"Yeah, I just… That was some heavy stuff."

"Is it ever not with my dad?" she said with a grin. "He told me to wait while he talked with you. Said he and I would chat sometime later tonight. Did he tell you anything important?"

"Yeah. We can talk more about it tomorrow; when we've got Andre safe and sound back at the cabin."

Jennifer placed a hand on Daniel's shoulder. "Hell yeah. I'll see you in that alley tomorrow. Try not to catch a stray while you're running to me, okay? I've stitched Andre up in plenty of strange locales but performing a medical procedure while driving a car isn't exactly in my training."

Daniel chuckled. "Sounds good. See you tomorrow."

Jennifer left. Daniel disrobed and fell into bed, smacking an empty can of beer off the nightstand to set his phone down. He tossed and turned for hours, anxiety plaguing his mind.

A beam of light streamed through the curtains, waking Daniel from a drool-soaked pillow about 15 minutes before his alarm. Stretching as he lifted himself out of bed, he took a series of deep breaths to calm his nerves. He dug through his closet to find the black sweatpants, T-shirt, and jacket he would wear to the job along with a homemade ski mask made from a black stocking cap. After tying his sneakers, he loaded his pistol, placing another cartridge of bullets in the zipped-up pocket of his jacket. The weight of the clip caused the pocket to hang low, but he figured nobody in the crowd would notice it as he approached.

He pulled the mask over his face and checked to make sure none of his facial features were visible. Holding the gun up to the mirror, his thoughts turned to Sarah for the first time in a long time. Would the Wendigo show up and do the same thing to him that it had done to her? To Soaring Eagle? Daniel rethought the idea more than a dozen times. This was a monumental risk he was taking. If it went south, both he and Andre could easily be killed. Then all this would have been for nothing. But the same would be true if he did nothing and left Andre's fate in the hands of the justice system, which would almost assuredly give him the death penalty, given the Wendigo's bloodlust.

Daniel took the mask off and stared at his face in the mirror. His beard was scraggly, and the light in his eyes that defined his youth was gone. And he was only in his 30s. Trauma can age a man at a breakneck speed, he thought. But he figured he didn't have too much longer to live, anyway.

Tucking the pistol into the holster strapped to his bare leg, Daniel checked himself up and down once more before departing. The mask was tucked in his pocket. He weaved through the crowd of travelers and casino patrons toward the exit of The Mirage.

For a moment, Daniel took in the subtle beauty of Las Vegas for what he thought might be the last time. It was a city that, for better or worse, defined American culture: excess, greed, selfishness, unbridled freedom to be an unrelenting piece of shit. Maybe Andre had a point about this whole socialism thing. Maybe in a system like that, workers in cities like Vegas wouldn't be tossed aside in favor of fat cat corporate blowhards. Guys like Reynolds wouldn't become successful or get possessed by power-hungry demons.

Daniel turned the corner toward the courthouse and saw a massive crowd already formed. Protestors on one side led by Christina and other local activists, with Reynolds's supporters on the other side waving Nevadan and American flags, screaming across the line. A red carpet was rolled out between them. As Daniel immersed himself among the protestors, he saw a limousine pull up. Reynolds (*Not Reynolds, the Wendigo*) emerged from the car and waved to the crowd with a wicked smile. Black veins squiggled up its neckline, and dark bags sat beneath its eyes, a husk of Reynolds's former self. Its skin seemed almost gray. The Wendigo walked, flanked by Reynolds's lawyers and security guards, without the help of a cane. It strolled along the line of diehard supporters, shaking hands and kissing babies. *God, help those babies avoid syphilis.*

An overwhelming urge overcame Daniel to pull out his gun and fire at the Wendigo. But that was Andre's mistake. No guarantee that he'd get a good shot at Reynolds's body, and there'd be no way to get Andre back from the authorities then. Besides, that obviously wouldn't kill the Wendigo. It was a death wish for Daniel and Andre. He had to think about the long term. He could kill this thing later.

Once the Wendigo entered the courthouse, a portion of Reynolds's supporters left. The full crowd of protestors remained, providing Daniel the cover he needed to go unrecognized. More of Reynolds's men arrived and entered the courthouse to provide him security. After another 10 minutes, a police van arrived. Two officers opened up the doors and led a handcuffed Andre out of the back. He had a beard, too, but it was a lot thicker than Daniel's. His hair was frizzed, and his face was thinner, sadder. The orange jumpsuit stood out against his dark skin.

"BOO! FUCK YOU!" Reynolds's remaining supporters yelled, spat and hurled objects at Andre, who barely flinched. He glared, though, and Daniel smiled, thinking about what Andre would do to some of the fat slobs in the crowd. If only he weren't wearing those handcuffs.

Daniel nodded to Christina, and the protestors began pushing against the barrier keeping them from Andre. One of the officers broke off from escorting Andre (*Perfect*) and tried to manage them. Daniel turned around, pulled on his mask, and turned back to charge him. He pulled out his gun and whipped the cop upside the head before leaping over the barrier. Daniel stumbled at the other officer, who was reaching for his sidearm, and fired two shots into his chest. It knocked the man back without leaving any bloody marks behind. *Bulletproof vest.*

The cop tried to wrestle himself back up, but Andre took advantage of the situation and stomped on his neck. He gagged on a crushed windpipe as Andre turned his eyes to Daniel. They widened. Daniel couldn't turn in time to see the first officer, who had recovered from his pistol whipping and tackled Daniel to the ground. The gun fell from Daniel's hand to Andre's feet. The barrel of a pistol pressed against the back of Daniel's head, and he heard a shot. Daniel didn't feel anything. He turned to his right and saw Andre, gun in his locked-up hands. The cop on Daniel's back fell to his left with a sopping red hole in the back of his skull.

"Time to go, Dan," Andre said. Even through a ski mask, Andre knew who he was. Daniel and Andre ran from the scene as Reynolds's supporters ran for their lives in the opposite direction. A handful of Reynolds's henchmen came barreling out of the courthouse and gave the duo chase, firing shots at their heels and above their heads. When Daniel glanced back, he saw the Wendigo standing near the entrance, its yellow eyes glowing in Reynolds's skull. It smiled.

Daniel shook off his fear and pointed to a nearby alley. Andre followed him, heavy footsteps and gunshots echoing behind them. Andre and Daniel turned a pair of corners, weaving between buildings, until they arrived at a black SUV with tinted windows. Jennifer kicked the passenger door open.

"Get in," she barked.

Daniel ripped open the back door and ushered Andre inside. "Lie down," he told him. Andre obliged, tucking himself on the floor behind the seats before Daniel shut the door. Daniel sat next to Jennifer, tore off his mask, and slammed his door. A bullet shattered Daniel's window and lodged itself in the headrest behind him with a *thunk.*

"Drive," he said. Jennifer sped out of the alley and headed north.

23

JENNIFER DROVE OVER A POTHOLE, causing Andre to bang his head on the underside of the driver's seat. His ears were still ringing from the gunshots in front of the courthouse.

"Ahh, fuck," Andre said. "Jenny, where'd you learn to drive?"

"Shut up," she replied. Andre rubbed the top of his head, his hands still bound together by the cuffs. They were chafing his wrists.

"Yo, Dan, can you get me out of these things? Bad enough I gotta squeeze my ass in here and keep bangin' my head and shit."

"Just wait until we get to the rez," Daniel said. "I don't exactly have a key on me."

"You don't need a key, bro. Just shoot 'em off."

Daniel turned back to Andre with a furrowed brow. "You want me to shoot a gun inside a moving car so you can be slightly more comfortable?"

Andre rolled his eyes and turned away from Daniel. He lay there in silence for the remainder of the ride, which became bumpier as they got closer to their destination. Relief overtook his anxiety as they got further from the city. When the car came to a stop, Andre sat up and kicked open the car door. On his way out, he tripped and fell onto the dusty ground. Daniel helped him up and brushed his shoulders off.

"That beard is looking pretty rough, man," Daniel said, putting his arm around Andre as they walked toward Soaring Eagle's old cabin.

"Least I'm still pretty. You ugly whether you shave or not."

Daniel chuckled. He led Andre to the side of the house where a pair of large hedge clippers were leaned against the wall. Daniel used them to split the chain on Andre's handcuffs. With a little jimmying using a rusty nail, Andre busted off the cuffs.

"Couple of innovators, you and I," Daniel said with a laugh.

"Yeah, no shit," Andre said as he followed Daniel and Jennifer inside the house. The place was tidy despite Soaring Eagle's passing. Andre figured Jennifer must have been keeping it up over the past few months. It felt strange for Andre to be somewhere normal again after all the time in his cell and the narrow halls of the jailhouse. The first thing he did was lay out on the couch and put his feet up, kicking off his shoes.

"No, it's okay, make yourself comfortable," Jennifer said. "You want a fucking foot massage, too?"

Andre perked up. "You don't wanna see what my toes be lookin' like. Hard to find nail clippers in the can."

Jennifer laughed. "Get off my couch and go get yourself cleaned up, man. There are some clothes in the guest room closet; help yourself to whatever fits. I'm gonna go talk to my dad."

Andre sat up, unsure of what he just heard. "Your dad?"

"Oh, shit," Daniel said. "Forgot to mention: Soaring Eagle's been communicating with us from the afterlife. Been talking to Jennifer and me through visions."

"Yo… That's wild. I *knew* he was like fuckin' Yoda."

Jennifer shook her head and left. Andre locked himself in the guest room. He peeled off his prison jumpsuit and underwear before strolling naked to the bathroom. He took a long look at himself in the mirror. His face was rough, dirty, hidden behind the beard. His hair was twisted and knotted in spots, longer than it had ever been. Chest hair was puffing out, too, and his pubic hair formed an afro of sorts above his low-hanging dick and balls. It all needed to be shaved. The clippers on the counter would have to perform full-body duty this afternoon. Then, Andre thought, it might be good to throw them away.

Andre hopped in the shower and washed himself. It was the first time he'd done so without looking over his shoulder for someone with a sharp object. He was never worried about the thing guys worry about when showering in jail in the movies—dropping the soap and all that—but the threat of violence did linger in his mind. Every activity was an anxious one for Andre in the slammer, especially after Reynolds and the Wendigo visited. White supremacists, psychotic murderers, ancient Native American demons; the fear of all of them lingering around the corner kept him on edge.

The shower at Soaring Eagle's place was soothing. Consistent hot water, fancy soaps all set up for the taking, a shampoo that tingled Andre's scalp. He took his time before drying off and getting to work on the overgrowth all over his body. Starting with the head and moving down, he shaved everything with the electric clippers on the bathroom counter. His head was down to a buzz cut, his beard was gone, his chest hair was minimal, and his pubes were tamed. Some work with the nail clippers and a file got his feet appearing respectable. He finally felt like himself again on the outside. Inside, trauma lingered. He wasn't sure who to trust anymore after his time behind bars. *Why did Dan wait so long?*

Boxers, sweatpants, and a NASA T-shirt made up Andre's borrowed outfit. He put on some fuzzy slippers, which felt like heaven on his blistered feet, and found Daniel. He was sitting at the dining room table where Andre first met Soaring Eagle. A brief twinge of sadness welled up in Andre's throat. He wished he'd saved the old man from the Wendigo, but at least he lived on as some kind of spirit.

"Well, well," Daniel said, breaking Andre out of his trance. "Look at you, man. You look like the Old Spice guy."

Lowering himself into the seat next to Daniel, Andre let out a sigh of relief. He felt comfortable for the first time in a long time. He put his hand on Daniel's shoulder.

"Good to be back, my man. Thanks for saving my ass."

With a smile, Daniel reached over and gave Andre a tight hug. Andre felt Daniel's phone buzz in his shirt pocket, which alarmed them both. Daniel stood and answered it.

"Hello?"

Andre wondered who was calling. *Gabby?*

"Uh-huh. Okay, wow… Are you serious?" Daniel said. His face went pale. *Even more pale than usual.* "Got it. I'll get back to you. Thanks for the heads up."

Daniel hung up and tossed the phone on the table. He put his hands on his head and paced around the room, appearing distraught.

"Dan, who the fuck was that?"

Daniel turned to him, worry on his face. "That was Oleg—one of Reynolds's men. He's been my guy on the inside since all this started."

"Holy shit. That's wild. What he say?"

"He said Reynolds is running for president. He's announcing it in two days at a rally on the Strip. Right down the street from his hotel."

"Yo… what?" Andre had chills. "Guy like that? President?"

Daniel sat next to Andre and leaned in close. "He's not just some guy anymore," Daniel said. "The Wendigo possessed Reynolds's body. It's all demon; no man left in there."

Andre considered the gravity of Daniel's words and decided his best friend needed reassurance right now, even if it took a longer time than he'd like to bust him out of jail. He patted him on the back.

"Dan, you know what we gotta do, right?"

Daniel turned to him. He seemed older than Andre remembered. His face had that sunken appearance that it did before the job with Sarah, only there were no stars in the sky for Andre to distract him with. Out the window, dark clouds formed over distant stretches of the desert.

In the dining room the next day, Andre sat around the table with Daniel, Jennifer, and Oleg, who'd driven up from downtown. Andre glared at Oleg.

"How we know you ain't gonna double-cross us?" he asked.

"You're right to be skeptical," Oleg said. "But trust me when I say this: I want Reynolds dead as much as the rest of you. In my time around him over the last few years, everything bad about him has only gotten worse."

Andre scoffed. "You knew who he was when you took the fuckin' job. Don't try and save face now, bro."

"I'm not saving face. This guy is a monster. It's not just the political stuff. Lately, he's been doing stuff that's just… inhuman. It's hard to explain, but he's… eating people. Cutting up bodies and eating them."

Nobody in the room other than Oleg seemed surprised or distraught.

"You guys know about this?" Oleg asked.

"It's not Reynolds driving this behavior," Jennifer said.

"Everything he's done over the last few months—running for office, the people he's killed, the ones he's consumed—it's been the influence of a demon my people call the Wendigo. It's in full control now. Reynolds is gone."

Andre was surprised to see Oleg nod in acceptance. Most of the people who heard this story so far didn't believe it at first, himself included.

"I've seen it come out of him," Oleg said. "Red skin, bright yellow eyes."

Jennifer perked up. "Did it say anything to you?"

"No. It just stared at me and smiled. This was a long time ago, before the election even. I haven't seen it in a long time."

Jennifer nodded. Oleg took advantage of the silence.

"Have you guys considered just having me shoot this thing in the head at his presidential announcement? I've thought about it a lot, and if I got close enough…"

"Lemme just stop you right there," Jennifer said. "Shooting Reynolds in the head won't kill the Wendigo. If we tried to do what you just described, it'd be way too dangerous. We're talking about assassinating a politician in broad daylight, here. Remember what happened when Andre tried that?"

"That's right," Daniel said. "We have to draw it out, do something to get it in an enclosed space, and then kill it the way Soaring Eagle said: with a silver blade to the heart."

"Whoa, whoa," Andre said. "Dan, ain't Soaring Eagle say we *can't* kill this motherfucker?"

"That's what he thought initially, yes." Daniel folded his hands. "But when I talked to him in a vision, he said his ancestors used a silver blade to kill this thing before. But we have to burn the heart after if we want to truly get rid of it."

"Man," Andre said, rubbing his temples. "This is a lot of shit to process, my guy."

"I know. But you remember the original job we planned,

right? The robbery? That's gonna be how we draw it out. Oleg told me a while back that he knows where the safes are."

Andre turned to Oleg, "You do?"

"Yes," Oleg said. "Since the election, he's had them under tight security in a back room at Energy Nightclub inside the hotel. Eight safes in all, holding almost $40 million."

Andre whistled. "That's more than we thought he had locked away. How the fuck we gonna get to it?"

"You and Daniel are going to have to fight your way in there," Oleg said. "The guys they normally have protecting it, I can make sure they're out of commission. But that Wendigo thing will likely send more of Reynolds's men after you. Your time will be limited."

Daniel sat forward, eyes locked on Andre. "We've gotta load those safes into industrial laundry bins and roll them out of there. Oleg, you get those set up for us and be there in time to help push the bins and provide cover."

"This sounds complicated as hell," Andre said, shaking his head. "And risky. You sure we can pull it off, just the three of us?"

"If we're quick, yes," Oleg said. "The trouble would be getting out to our vehicle. We might be under fire."

Daniel pointed at Jennifer. "This is where you come in," he said. "We need you to drive the getaway car like you did yesterday. You help load the safes in the back of that big SUV, and we hightail it out of there."

"That's all good by me," she said. "But Daniel, you're forgetting something."

Jennifer tossed four knives on the table. *Silver. Hell yeah.* Andre, Daniel, and Oleg each grabbed one and examined it. Andre's brown eyes reflected off the surface. Engraved in each wooden handle was an eagle snatching a mouse in its talons.

"A craftsman in town did these for me yesterday," Jennifer

said, lifting up her knife. "Custom. Sterling silver. Close enough to pure silver to do the job."

Andre practiced a stabbing motion with clenched teeth. Daniel laughed.

"If the Wendigo comes for you," Jennifer said, pointing to her chest. "Aim for the fucking heart."

24

D ANIEL JAMMED HIS CIGARETTE INTO the ashtray and gazed at the sunset. The orange glow of the on-coming night brought him momentary peace. But anxiety returned, as it always did, wrapping its tendrils around his mind. He thought about Gabby—how their last conversation was a yelling match over the phone; how he'd never touch her again. How he might be better off wandering into the desert and dying of thirst than being killed by the Wendigo.

With a deep breath of cold air through his nose, Daniel shook off his thoughts and returned to the living room in Soaring Eagle's cabin, where Andre was loading a pistol. Andre handed Daniel a Beretta M9.

"Thanks. Loaded?"

"Nah, it's just blanks," Andre said with a snicker. "Fuck you think, dumbass?"

"Sorry. Just want to be sure. This is some high-risk shit."

"Dan, I know you talk when you get nervous, but try shuttin' the fuck up for a few minutes."

Jennifer came into the room in a plaid long-sleeve shirt tucked into jeans, along with an oversized belt buckle. Wrapped across her chest in a sling was a shotgun; she had bullets tucked into her front pocket. A white feather stuck out from her black cowboy hat.

"Damn," Andre said. "Jenny comin' with the *heat*."

"'Failing to prepare is preparing to fail,'" she said. "That's what my old man liked to say, anyway."

"He was right," Daniel said. "But what's with the cowboy get up?"

"I feel comfortable in this. I don't need to be inconspicuous like you guys. Don't worry, I won't spit tobacco or hoot and holler at any passing ladies."

Andre laughed. "You wild. Glad we got somebody ridin' heavy for when we get out there. I still don't feel like we got enough time to get all them safes in the back of that truck."

"Do you know how to use that thing?" Daniel asked Jennifer. She frowned.

"Do I know how to use this thing? Daniel, I think you're forgetting: I grew up in rural America just as much as those White boys who love Reynolds, and my neck's just as red. Some would say it's even redder."

Daniel chuckled. He tucked the silver knife into a holster on his belt and made sure it was secure. He would need it for the Wendigo. The situation had played out in his mind all last night. Andre would be the aggressor, and Daniel would have to jump in and save him, plunging the knife into Reynolds's rotten chest and killing the demon inside. Daniel would have to skip town, sure, but he'd be a hero.

"Guys," Daniel said. "I've got something I need to tell you both before we do this."

Daniel leaned against the wall by the TV. Jennifer and Andre sat next to each other on the couch, listening with concern on their faces.

"After this is over and we get the money out of those safes, I won't be sticking around for the aftermath. I've got a place in

Montana that I've put a deposit on: cabin in the woods, far away from the heat we're about to feel. You guys can come with me if you want for a while, just until things cool off."

Andre's eyes darted around the room, as if searching for the right words. Jennifer stood up.

"I'm staying here with my wife and kid," she said. "They need me. And if we do this right, nobody will come snooping around the reservation, anyway."

Daniel turned to Andre who refused to meet his gaze.

"Andre?"

"Dan," he said, leaning back into the couch and staring at the ceiling. "I can't come with you, bro. That kind of life ain't for me. I'll come up and visit one day, but you on your own out there. You'll have plenty of money to hold you down, right?"

Daniel laughed through the pain in the pit of his stomach. "Yeah, I think $10 million will do me good."

Andre stood and headed for the door, but Daniel stopped him to reach out for a hug. They embraced after a decade of close calls. One call to go.

"I'll go grab the van and pull around front," Jennifer said.

Daniel and Andre stood and watched the clear night come into focus, stars dotting the spaces not polluted by the city lights. If he stared straight up, Daniel could see them more clearly; they were obscured by the city's glow on the edge of the horizon.

"So what you gonna do with all that money?" Andre asked.

"After I buy the house? Not sure. You?"

"I been thinkin' about opening a drive-in theater," Andre said. Daniel's eyebrows raised. "Show classic movies and shit, but new ones, too. *Dre's Drive-In*. Imagine how fuckin' dope it would be to watch movies every night. No lookin' over my shoulder or chasing demons and shit. Just the beauty of the cinema."

Daniel smiled. "Sounds like a hell of a plan, brother."

Jennifer pulled up, and her headlights blinded Daniel for a moment.

Daniel absorbed the neon hum of the Las Vegas Strip. The van sped through the center of town, but not too fast to avoid attracting attention. Jennifer pulled up to The Luxury and turned back to Andre and Daniel in the back seat.

"You guys ready?"

"As we'll ever be," Daniel said. He and Andre bumped fists and went out either side of the van, slamming the doors in near unison. Outside the hotel, sweat forming on his wrinkled brow, was Oleg.

"Yo, Oleg," Andre said. "You just get in a workout before this?"

"No," Oleg said with heavy breath. "I had to rush out here. Was running a bit behind schedule. Had to turn off those security cameras, too."

"Well," Daniel said, placing a hand on his shoulder. "We're glad you made it."

Oleg led Daniel and Andre through the crowded casino and back to the nightclub where a line of patrons waited behind a red velvet rope: men and women in cheap dresses and dress shirts, slicked hair and caked makeup, ready for a night of overpriced joy.

Daniel's nerves built as they approached the entrance, but the security guard waved them through without a second glance once he saw Oleg. Stepping into the heart of Energy Nightclub, bass reverberated in Daniel's chest and neon lights flashed in every direction. Bodies gyrated on the floor, surrounded by booths with leather couches. Strong drinks in small glasses sat on each table. Those sitting in roped-off areas were smoking cigars and gazing leerily around the room. They were undoubtedly the criminal types Reynolds associated with.

Daniel and Andre arrived at their booth, and Oleg moved the rope for Andre and Daniel. "I'll meet you guys down there in five," he said. "Don't look at anybody the wrong way."

The high-pitched croons of an R&B artist echoed underneath the bass. Andre was nodding his head. Women on the dance floor shook their asses, some up to the belts of the men they were with.

"Yo," Andre yelled over the music, "this shit slaps."

Daniel nodded. He couldn't focus on the music—eyes, watching him from above, were boring holes in the back of his head. He turned up to the private rooms overlooking the dance floor with clear glass windows that could be custom tinted to the VIP guest's liking. All were dark but one. Standing in the window staring down at them was the Wendigo in Reynolds's body. Its eyes glowed. Nobody was paying attention but Daniel.

"Andre," he said, grabbing him by the shirt, "look up there."

When he turned back, the Wendigo was no longer there. Andre smacked Daniel's hand away.

"Yeah, what?" Andre said, rubbing the wrinkled portion of his shirt flat. "You fucked up my 'fit, bro."

"Fuck your 'fit. I just saw the fucking Wendigo."

"Nigga, what? Where?"

"Up there, in that VIP suite. It… it's gone now."

"Shit, aight," Andre said, checking his watch. "I'll keep my eye out, but we gotta get down there. It's now or never."

Daniel might have preferred never. He followed Andre to the back door, which Oleg had propped open so they could enter without issue. Checking to make sure nobody was following them, Daniel slid through the door behind Andre and let it shut. They hustled down a dark hallway to the stairwell, and as Daniel took the left, he saw a light flash out of the corner of his eye. He stopped.

"Dan," Andre whispered. "Get a move on. Let's go."

Daniel was transfixed by the swinging light fixture down the hall, its spotlight dragging from wall to wall. It slowed down and came to a stop. The Wendigo stood beneath the light, only it was no longer in Reynolds's body. For the first time, he saw it in its true form: red skin, triangular face, black veins, yellow eyes, gnashing teeth. A wicked stench lingered in Daniel's nostrils. Daniel raised his gun, but the light went out. He ran after Andre who was already halfway down the stairs.

"Andre!" Daniel yelled. "Wait up. I just saw it again."

"Shit, what?" Andre said, turning back and waiting for Daniel to catch up. Once they were next to each other, they hoofed it step for step to the basement door. Daniel swung it open, and Andre entered, gun raised. Daniel watched him lower it and run down the hall. Oleg was waiting for both of them, laundry bins waiting for their cargo of safes. Two corpses lay on the floor. Andre kicked one of them as he passed by.

"Hurry up," Oleg said. "Let's get a few loaded before backup gets here."

"Why did you kick that guy?" Daniel asked Andre.

"That's the dude that beat my ass at the rally." Andre spat on the hefty Black man's face. An exit wound oozed below his left eye next to Andre's loogie. "Tyson was his name. Glad that motherfucker's dead."

Daniel followed Andre and Oleg to the safes, which were stacked in a dusty room beneath an old, creaking lamp, similar to the one Daniel saw above the Wendigo moments before. Daniel struggled to help Andre lift a safe and lower it into the laundry bin. Then another. His lower back ached. On the third safe, footsteps echoed from the hallway. *Party's here.*

Oleg reloaded his gun while Daniel and Andre hurried to the door. They leaned out into the hallway and fired shots toward their pursuers. One collapsed while another flinched from a shoulder wound. The wounded gunman fired into the darkness. A bullet whizzed by Daniel's head. Andre leaned out behind Daniel and fired a few more. They made contact with the man's chest, and he crumpled.

Two more were coming from behind Daniel, their feet clopping on the concrete floors. He slid out behind the laundry basket and reloaded, sucking in a breath before turning to unload his clip. Both of Reynolds's men took rounds to the chest. The one who survived leaned up from his stomach to fire two rounds. A bullet hit Andre in the leg, and he winced, falling next to Daniel.

"Shit," Andre said, grabbing at his ankle. Blood stained his fingers. Daniel stood up straight and walked with purpose toward the shooter, who was gurgling and trying to reload his gun. It slipped out of the man's hands, and he looked up at Daniel's arrival. Daniel fired one in the grunt's skull. Another came screaming around the corner, and Daniel filled him with lead. Silence, save for Andre's groaning.

"Andre!" Daniel yelled back. "You good?"

"Yeah," he said, pushing himself to his feet. He limped over to the wall, leaning against it and sliding down. "This shit ain't bleeding much."

Daniel jogged over to Andre. As he stared at Andre's wound, cold air washed over the back of Daniel's neck. *Where the fuck is Oleg?*

Daniel saw him. Floating. Down the hallway. He was clutching at his neck. Out of the darkness stepped the Wendigo. A massive red arm extending from Reynolds's torn shirtsleeve choked out Oleg. The rest of the body was Reynolds. It seemed like it couldn't figure out which form it wanted to take.

Oleg's neck snapped. The arm dropped his corpse to the floor. Daniel reached for his gun out of instinct but figured it would be of no use. He snagged the knife instead and ran at the Wendigo.

His feet left the floor and he flew into the wall, smacking his head against the concrete.

The Wendigo laughed in Reynolds's voice. "Oh, man, you should've seen your face. Pulling the tough guy act and shit. Should I make myself look like that woman again? Come nurse your wound?"

Daniel's vision was hazy. The back of his head was hot. He touched it and saw blood on his hand. The Wendigo walked at a casual pace toward him, its body growing and contracting between a vague shape of Reynolds and a large, gangly beast. Daniel shuddered.

"You fucking fool," it said in its true voice: deep, scratchy. "You thought you could come in here and take *my* money out from under my nose? You know what I'll do with this, don't you?"

It stood above Daniel and glared behind a human face. Black veins wiggled up Reynolds's neck. It leaned close to Daniel as he clutched for the knife, stepping on his hand before he could reach it.

"I'm going to take this money and put it into my presidential run," the Wendigo said. "And once these foolish people put me in office, I will bring suffering the likes of which man has not yet seen. I will feast on the innards of the weak; bathe myself in the blood of the innocent."

Daniel felt his hand going numb. He heard slow footsteps coming his direction: a foot dragging on the floor. The Wendigo turned to its right. Daniel's eyes followed.

Andre limped toward the Wendigo, clutching his own silver knife. He was inching closer but didn't seem to be going fast enough. The Wendigo lifted its foot from Daniel's hand.

"What did I tell you before, Andre?" the Wendigo said. "I don't want to kill you. I'd rather watch you rot."

"Only one of us gonna be rottin', motherfucker," Andre spat back, dragging himself closer.

Through the haze filling his field of vision, Daniel snatched the knife from the floor and swung it blindly at the Wendigo. He heard a slice. It clutched at its ankle and fell to one knee, crying out in pain. Daniel saw Andre make his move and thought there might have been an opening for his best friend to deliver a final strike. But why did it have to be him? Andre lifted his right arm, but it froze mid-stab.

The knife inches from its chest, the Wendigo gripped Andre's arm with a red, clawed hand, black veins pulsating. Its eyes glowed brighter.

"Well," it said, Reynolds's voice now, "you really fucked that one up, didn't ya?"

The Wendigo pulled Andre back and tossed him across the room. A snap echoed in the basement hallway. In the Wendigo's massive hand was Andre's severed arm, maintaining a death grip on the knife. It stared at the limb under the light, cackling. Across the hall, Andre screamed, rolling and clutching at the bloody stump below his right shoulder. Daniel tried to push himself up but was knocked back again.

Ripping through Reynolds's old clothes with its bulging red arms, the Wendigo turned to Daniel and flashed its rotten teeth. It took a satisfied bite of Andre's arm like it was eloté at the state fair. It licked the blood and muscle tissue off its long fingers with a forked tongue. Daniel watched its eyes go black as it lifted a claw in the air.

A crunch echoed through the hallway. The Wendigo was frozen with its arms up.

Daniel's eyes darted to his right: Jennifer, thrusting the silver blade into the side of the Wendigo's chest, just below its armpit. It shrieked, causing Daniel to briefly lose his hearing. He watched the monster swing its arms wildly, shrink down to human size and revert to Reynolds's form. The old man's body fell to the floor as Jennifer twisted her arm into the large wound, yanking the black heart from Reynolds's chest with surgical precision. Red veins pulsated on the dark organ as blood ran through her fingers.

"Come on," Jennifer said, extending her free hand to help Daniel up. "We've got to go."

Daniel stood and began to run alongside her. They arrived at Andre, whose screams hadn't ceased, and worked together to lift him into the laundry basket. Warm blood ran down Daniel's back from Andre's ghastly shoulder stump. He lowered him into the laundry basket along with three of the safes and pushed with all his strength toward the service elevator. Jennifer put the Wendigo's heart in a burlap bag and cocked her shotgun.

The elevator went up in a flash, Daniel processing the moment with a blank stare until the doors slid open. More of Reynolds's men. He realized he'd forgotten his weapon in the basement. Jennifer fired at one of the men and blew his head off, freezing for a moment after she did it. The other was deafened by the sound and soon received the butt of the gun to the front of his skull. He collapsed out of the way.

"Let's go!" Jennifer yelled. "Car's out front."

They made it to the vehicle without chase, loading the safes in the trunk and helping Andre into the backseat. He groaned, delirious, losing blood fast.

"There they are!"

Daniel turned back toward the front door: three men in suits, only one with a gun. Daniel tore the shotgun from Jennifer's grasp and ran at the trio, firing into the gunman's knees. He collapsed without a left kneecap and dropped his weapon. His unarmed compatriots scurried off in fear.

Jennifer was already in the driver's seat twisting the keys by the time Daniel turned back around. The engine purred.

"Get—"

"Get in," Daniel said with an exhale. "Yeah. No shit."

25

K NEELING BESIDE ANDRE'S BED, DANIEL wept. He knew he'd have to leave before his friend ever woke up… *if* he woke up. No proper goodbye either way. What a shitty sendoff. Daniel repeatedly punched a hole in the drywall until he saw red streaks in the white, chalky mess.

Blood dripped from his knuckles as Daniel pushed himself up and wiped away tears, refusing to turn back to the bed and look at Andre again. It had been less than 24 hours since the robbery and the pain in the back of his head lingered. Jennifer evaluated him for a concussion and determined he was fine, but he still felt hazy. Perhaps watching Andre's wound get cauterized with a blowtorch in the back of a barn, horses screaming over the crackling sound, was too much for him.

In the living room of Soaring Eagle's cabin, Jennifer was watching TV with a cup of coffee in her shaking hand. She'd been keeping up with the news of what the public thought was Reynolds's assassination. No leads yet, and already theories from pundits about left-wing activists being responsible. Or Mexican drug cartels, given the gruesome detail of a missing heart. Little did the people know the horrors they'd been saved from, Daniel thought. For a reason he couldn't place, it angered Daniel that he

wasn't the one to strike the fatal blow. He resented even looking at Jennifer, who was behaving far too casually for someone
who'd just killed an ancient demon.

"Hey," Jennifer said. "You want coffee?"

"Nah," Daniel said, sinking into an armchair. He pulled out a
cigarette and sparked it up in his hands, his shaking too. Jennifer
seemed to pick up on their shared struggle.

"Do you want to meditate?" she asked. Daniel scoffed at the
idea.

"Is your dad going to use his magic powers to wake up Andre?" Daniel spat. He took a long drag on the cigarette and blew
smoke up toward the ceiling fan. Jennifer grimaced.

"Could you please not smoke in here?" she asked. Daniel
yanked the cigarette from his mouth and crushed it in his fist. He
let it burn his palm and glared at her.

"So is my money ready to go?"

"Yes," Jennifer said. "It's in a duffel bag in the guest room. I
already packed up your suitcases in the car for you."

"Is it all there?"

"Yep. Five million in total for you, a three-way split of the
fifteen million we were able to escape with."

"And what if Andre doesn't wake up? What about his
money?"

Jennifer seemed offended by the question, as if Daniel had
no hope left for Andre. He wasn't sure if he did.

"*If* he doesn't wake up," she said. "I'll split it in half and
bring you your share myself. Think of it as one more house call."

Daniel ignored the attempt at humor, nodded, and started
for the guest room. He stopped when he heard Jennifer speak up
again, her tone softer.

"Daniel?"

He turned back, rage still bubbling in his gut. "What?"

"How do you deal with it? Killing people? I just can't get

the picture out of my mind of the one guy's head missing its top half… because of me. I've seen dead bodies at work before, but never—"

"Never like that?"

Jennifer nodded. Her hands began to shake again under the coffee mug. "Yes."

Daniel sighed. "You want the truth? It was either them or us. The longer we waited or the less willing we were to get violent, the more likely it was that we ended up with a hole in *our* heads."

Jennifer's eyes darted around. "But like… how do you deal with it? The guilt?"

Daniel remained stone faced. He walked over to Jennifer and stared at her, feeling nothing.

"There can't be any guilt," he said. "Just move on with your fucking life. They're dead, and you're not. If you need to feel better about it, think about all the people who are better off now that the Wendigo's dead. Those guys you shot, they were just collateral."

Jennifer didn't seem sure of Daniel's advice. He didn't care. On the bed in the guest room was the duffel bag with his blood money. He returned to the room, swung it over his shoulder and headed for the front door. Jennifer stopped him.

"Here," she said, handing him a small wooden box. It was varnished with an engraving of a large feather across the top. Daniel recognized it. Soaring Eagle kept his pipe in there.

"Your dad's pipe?"

"No. I took that out. This is the Wendigo's heart."

"What the hell?" Daniel asked, handing the box back in a rush. "The fuck are you giving me that for? You didn't burn it?"

"It has to be you. My dad said the person who strikes the blade can't be the one to strike the match. You have to burn it when you get to Montana."

Daniel wondered if he wanted that responsibility. But it gave him a sliver of satisfaction to think that he had the power to rid the world of the Wendigo for good. Pittance for not being able to stab the motherfucker himself. He snatched the box from Jennifer's hand and turned the doorknob.

"Thanks," he said.

Jennifer rushed to Daniel and gave him a hug. "Good luck out there. Give me a call once you're settled and once you burn that thing."

Daniel nodded despondently as they pushed apart. Jennifer shut the door behind him.

Parked on the side of the house was Andre's Mercedes. If Andre lived, he'd pay him back somehow, with an even better ride. Daniel tossed the duffel bag in the trunk and placed the box with the Wendigo's heart carefully on the passenger's seat. He turned the key, and the engine roared to life.

Up a winding back road in a forest of ponderosa pines, Daniel had his window cracked and breathed in the fresh air. Just a mile or so from his new home. Twelve hours, give or take, he'd been driving with stops only for gas, relieving himself, and food—all with his face covered in case the authorities named him a suspect. But he hadn't heard anything yet, not even on national radio stations covering the assassination.

Daniel pulled up to the cabin under the moonlight; silence except for a hooting owl. He got out of the car, stretched, and observed his new home. He grabbed the keys from the glove box and headed for the front door to check the cabin out before unpacking.

The inside was refurbished, with a modern feel that provided a nod to classic log cabin décor; hand-woven pillows on couches with tan fabric, lacquered wood tables, and a TV stand built from dark logs without a speck of dust; enough room for more than just Daniel and his thoughts. He thought about getting a dog to keep him company—a Labrador, like his family had growing up in Sacramento.

A note from the previous owner sat on the coffee table addressing Daniel's pseudonym:

> *Robert,*
> *Welcome to your new home. Firewood is in the shed along with tools for landscaping. Call us with questions. Enjoy this new adventure!*
> *- Stacy and Mark McNeil*

Daniel crumpled up the note and shoved it in his pocket. He returned to the car and unloaded his belongings, carrying them to the back bedroom. Dropping the final bag on his bed, he stared out the sliding glass door to the expanse of his yard. *I could use a smoke.*

Sliding the door open, he stepped out on the back porch and lit one up. The air was different here, he thought, free from the stench and grime of the city he'd come to know like the back of his hand. Only problem with rural Montana, he thought, was the lack of available prostitutes. No index cards with nude photos scattered on the forest floor. If he were to find a girl up here, she'd know him only as Robert Reed from Oregon, a former insurance salesman looking for a simple life in the heartland. The idea of playing that part made him laugh as he put out the last nub of his cigarette.

Daniel thought of Andre as he rounded the cabin back to the car: how uncomfortable he'd be in this space, and how much fun the two of them would have adjusting to ranch life after robbing, killing, and hustling for so long. The absence of his presence in Daniel's life made him feel emptier than ever before. He wondered if depression would set in before he could buy a dog;

nothing to stop him from blowing his brains out right then, if he wanted to.

Shaking the thought, Daniel swung open the passenger door of Andre's car and grabbed the box with the Wendigo's heart, carrying it with him to the shed on the side of his cabin. He collected firewood, a flint, and some old newspapers. It didn't take long before a fire was set up in his front yard, its orange flicker warming Daniel's body as the early spring cold snap blew through the forest. Daniel thought about Sarah, Soaring Eagle and Andre; about the blackness in the Wendigo's eyes just before Jennifer stabbed it in the chest.

Flicking a cigarette aside, Daniel reached for the wooden box with the feather across its surface. He rubbed his thumb along the engraving before pulling off the lid.

It was empty.

A large red hand unfolded its bony fingers on his shoulder.

Acknowledgments

A special thanks to beta-readers Kaelen Jones, H.D. Hastilow, and Julia Skinner — along with the critiquing community on Scribophile — for their edits, guidance, and support throughout the writing process. Thank you to Abel "The Weeknd" Tesfaye for providing the creative inspiration for this novel through his life-changing album, *After Hours*, which also served as the soundtrack to writing each chapter.

This story is far from over…

About the Author

RYAN CLARKE is a journalist and author born and raised in Beaverton, Oregon, although he will claim Portland whenever anyone asks where he's from. After graduating from Arizona State University in 2018, he has worked as a sports and news reporter for The Bulletin and The Newberg Graphic, both newspapers in his home state. When he isn't writing, he enjoys a glass (or two, or three) of Oregon Pinot noir, caring for his eccentric labradoodle, Porter, and watching horror movies that shock the conscience. *Obscurity* is his debut novel.